Garland's Christmas Romance

A Peter Pan-inspired Contemporary Romance Novella

by

Danielle Thorne

CHAPTER ONE

The tall stranger she noticed at the corner bistro table raised a hand when she strode past him to clear an empty teacup from the window seat. "Miss?"

"Just a minute," Garland Tate called back, raising her voice so that it would carry over the holiday music. Lunchtime was the busiest shift of the day even though the Lava Java café only served finger sandwiches and pastries. They needed the business.

Garland wiped down the seat and tabletop as she looked out of the plate glass window over the street. The hide-and-seek sunshine had disappeared for good above the cloud cover.

"Excuse me?"

She halted in mid-stride on her way back to the kitchen. "Yes?" Garland tried to hide the impatience in her tone. Tall, Fair, and Handsome had a plastic number card on his table which meant his food would be brought out when it was ready.

"Could you check on my order?"

"Twenty-seven?"

He glanced at his order number and nodded. "Thank you. I've been here almost a half-hour."

There was a crispness to his voice, a hint of an accent, but she couldn't place it. Australia? New Zealand? He didn't sound irritated or rude, but something about him exasperated her. "Yes, I'll check on it, Mister...?"

"Darling." He said it in a smooth tone, and she almost stepped back at his nerve.

"Excuse me?" Garland felt her shields go up. She didn't have time for flirting.

"Mr. Darling. Pete."

"Oh." The little hiccup in her pulse adjusted itself. He wasn't hitting on her. Darling was his name. "Yes, Mr. Darling, I'll check on your order." She looked sideways at him on her way to the front counter where the line for coffee, tea, and cocoa looked impossibly longer.

Garland pushed through the crowd to the register. "Mariah? Do you have the order for twenty-seven?"

Her boss pointed at the service counter and scanned it with her finger. "Twenty-four, six, nine... No, not yet. Let me check on that."

Garland picked up two orders that were ready, gave Mariah a quick nod, and dashed back out onto the floor. She felt Pete Darling's piercing eyes on her as soon as she left the counter.

"It's coming," she announced when he drew a breath to say something to her. She delivered orders twenty-four and twenty-six, greeted her favorite customer, Rhea, at the corner table tapping away on her laptop, and then dashed back to the kitchen.

She couldn't help but glance sideways at the man in the expensive-looking shirt when she hurried past his seat again. He still watched her like she was a specimen under a microscope.

With a shiver of annoyance, Garland hurried back to the kitchen and found Doug, the high school grad, coaching the panini machine like it was in labor.

"We still need order twenty-seven." She walked over and pulled the ticket clipped over the service window to see what the pushy man wanted.

A Ginger Volcano? Garland let out a long exhale when she saw the order for a deluxe cocoa with caramel, whipped cream, gingerbread cookie crumbles, and sprinkles. The front counter was so swamped they just hadn't had time. He'd also ordered a piece of cinnamon toast which was a rare request, not to mention, inconvenient. *Sugar junkie.*

"I've got twenty-seven," she called to Mariah. The manager at the register nodded.

Garland buttered and seasoned a large slice of homemade bread from the bakery. It was less than a week after Thanksgiving, but the town of Thorpes had flipped the page to the next chapter: Christmas. Hoping the bread didn't burn, she darted back out to the coffee counter. Steam from the hot water machine made spirals in the air as lava-hot water hit the powdered cocoa and sugar.

She almost resented the gingerbread beverage. It meant it was the end of another year, and now everyone's focus was on a tacky, over-colored, over-scented, and over-hyped holiday to celebrate wasting money on things that didn't matter. A *splish!* of hot cocoa bounced out of the hefty mug and burned her hand. She winced. She needed every penny she made working to pay off tuition. Now that's what mattered.

"Miss?"

She knew his voice by now. If she hadn't been holding a cup of volcanic hot chocolate she would have spun around and shouted, "What?"

Ignoring Pete Darling, whom she guessed was leaning over the other side of the counter eyeballing her, she picked up a bottle of caramel and gave the hot drink a squirt, then she looked.

He indeed stood across from her, staring as she suspected, but with his hands in his pockets.

"I told you it'd be ready in a minute. We're a little short-staffed today."

"I understand." The politeness irritated her. His smile made him look like a mischievous but innocent little boy.

She reached for the whipped cream and made a pretty cloud of cream and sugar. Pete's steady gaze made her self-conscious. "If you'd like to take a seat, I'll bring it out in a moment." She forced her tone not to sound like a drill sergeant.

Bright eyes glistened in the warm lighting of the café's canned lights. "I don't mind picking it up. I can see you're busy."

Garland ignored him. She reached for the cookie crumbles, sprinkled over a generous spoonful, and then added the sprinkles.

"That's very Christmas-y," he said conversationally.

"Yes," she answered, "and a bit early since it won't be December for five more days."

Pete Darling folded his arms on the counter. "I couldn't help myself. It already looks wintry here with all of the frozen dew, and I think I saw a flurry of snowflakes this morning."

Garland finished off the beverage with red and green sprinkles. She almost asked him where he was from since he thought snowfall was something to be excited about, but she forced herself not to encourage anymore small talk. "Here you go." She pushed it across the counter toward him. "I'll bring your toast out in a second."

"Thanks, Garland." He winked at her, picked up the steaming mug, and maneuvered carefully through the seats back to his table.

She stared after him then down at her apron to make sure she wasn't wearing a nametag. Another ripple of consternation hopscotched down her spine. She frowned, returned to the kitchen toaster, slipped out the cinnamon-coated bread, and arranged it on a plate. Grabbing another order, she strode out and delivered cookies to the librarian sitting next to Rhea, then walked across the room to Pete.

He stared out the front window now instead of at her, blowing over the top of the mug and watching something across the street.

Garland followed his gaze. A wintry mix of rain and slush spattered the sidewalks and streets. It would be icy on her way to class tonight, but she needed the good grades. She frowned, wondering why she'd put up with Thorpes' Icelandic weather for so long and dropped the plate onto Darling's table with a rattle. "Here's your toast."

His gaze darted up to her, and she felt her stomach plummet a few stories down. She forced it to stop on the landing of common sense. His eyes were blue-green as if they couldn't decide what color they wanted to be, and under the reflection of the faux lantern glowing on his table, she realized his hair was not as dark as it first seemed but had reddish highlights.

"Thank you," he said. There was something so personal about the way he searched her eyes when their gazes met that warning bells sounded in the back of her mind. She didn't know this man. She'd never seen him in her life, but he acted like he was a regular that came in every day.

"Hey," she said, stepping back to shake off a trance, "how do you know my name?"

The cheerful creases around his mouth seemed to stiffen into position. "You weren't supposed to know I knew your name."

The mental alarm bells began to ring again. "Well, that's not creepy," she joked, but she meant it, and she made sure he knew it, too.

Pete glanced down at the toast like he wanted to eat it. "I just recognized you is all."

He picked it up and took a bite, dismissing her, but she stayed rooted to the floor. If this was some weirdo from her college campus or social media, it'd be better to find out now before she ended up in a ditch somewhere along the New England coast.

"From where?" She made sure he heard the insistent tone in her voice. "'Fess up now, buddy, before I kick you out and call the cops. Where do you know me from?"

She watched him chew slowly, smile at her in hopes she'd give up and go away, and then finally took a dramatic swallow.

Garland folded her arms so she didn't put her hands on her hips. Time was money, and he was wasting hers.

"I heard someone call you by name up at the counter," he said. "That's all."

"Oh." She'd have to analyze his reply later because it caught her off-guard.

"Garland! Another Gingerbread Volcano, please!"

She swung her attention back toward the counter where Mariah had the crowd under control but was in need of her special skills. Garland felt silly. Of course, he'd probably heard someone else say her name.

She threw Pete a curious look. "Darling was my grandfather's and my mother's surnames." She tried to keep the accusation out of her voice, but something about this stranger struck a weird vibe with her.

"Oh?"

She observed his reaction and guessed from the frozen smile that he wasn't surprised.

"Garland?" Her boss sounded desperate now. She swung her head back toward Mariah and nodded then turned back to the stranger.

"See, you started something. Another Gingerbread Volcano order. I'll be back in a minute." She made sure he heard the warning in her voice.

Dashing back to the bar to make the drink, her mind bounced back and forth like a tennis ball between beverage orders and the curious man in the corner. When she finally pushed the to-go order over to the waiting customer, she mumbled, "Merry Christmas," but only because Mariah was within earshot.

Finally free, Garland tossed a towel onto the counter and slipped through the crowd of customers back to the corner bistro seat. Pete Darling was gone. She stopped in front of the table in surprise and examined his half-eaten toast. He'd only taken one bite and drank half the cocoa before he'd left. She glanced up toward the restrooms, but the door to the gentlemen's room was ajar, and the lights were off.

Scrunching her forehead, Garland turned toward the window. Heavy raindrops had turned to sleet, blowing at an angle down Main Street. She watched a few people dash past the café outside with their heads bowed to keep the needle-sharp ice out of their eyes.

"Perfect," she groused, wondering if there would be snow tomorrow. They'd already endured short-lived flurries off and on for weeks. Hopefully, when she graduated college and escaped Thorpes it'd be somewhere with less snow—and holiday enthusiasm. With a furrowed brow, she returned to the counter and tried to shake the feeling of *déjà vu* Pete Darling had cast over her day.

He'd left without finishing the order he wanted so badly. Odd. She'd mentioned her grandfather was a Darling, and he'd disappeared as fast as a Thorpes sunny day in December. If he did have family around, she'd never heard of him, but then again, Grandpa and Great Aunt Grace had been born and raised in England until they were seven and eight.

Garland knew all of the Darlings in Thorpes. The well-dressed and suave Pete Darling wasn't one of them.

PETE BRACED HIMSELF against cold splinters of ice as he dashed two doors down to the post office parking lot where he'd left the car. He hadn't expected Garland Tate to make the connection, but then again, he hadn't expected to find a beauty that made his heart cartwheel in slow motion the first moment he laid eyes on her. She'd no sooner mentioned her grandfather, Wendy Darling's son, and he realized he should leave. He wasn't prepared for any further conversation. She couldn't know the truth.

No one had noticed he'd parked at the post office after dropping off his mail, and he breathed an inward sigh of relief that he hadn't been towed. Not that he expected to be towed in a town like Thorpes. He'd recognized the charm of the New England village as soon as he'd passed the hand-painted town limits sign the first time he'd passed through years ago. The guardrails along the highway were wooden beams instead of metal. Black lampposts with iron scrollwork lined the sidewalks into town. All of the buildings were traditional brick and flat-faced, with pitched roofs to handle bucketloads of snow. At this time of year, Main Street glimmered with red and green early Christmas decorations.

He smiled to himself as he slipped into his electric car with a touch of the door handle. It was still warm inside. "Nibs," he said out loud to the smart system, "what's the time?"

A playful young boy's voice said, "It's 1:15, Pete!"

He pulled out of the post office parking lot in his expensive toy and headed for his new quarters. The Blackberry Inn stood a mile down the road and a block west of Main Street. Pete eased the car down the wet road. Traffic had eased considerably since lunchtime, but he imagined the weather had encouraged people to hurry home.

"Is it going to snow tonight, Nibs?" He glanced up at the overcast sky and slushy drizzle hitting the windshield.

"There's a thirty-five percent chance."

To be in town for the first real snowfall would be wonderful. Pete could hardly remember snow from when he was a small child. It never fell in Miami. These days, the holidays with its lights and presents and snow were some of his favorite things although he still felt like an outsider. He'd given up many things to grow up, but Christmas wasn't one of them.

The self-driving car slowed itself, and Pete watched the steering wheel spin eerily to the right as it guided the vehicle into the Inn's driveway. He hit a switch and took over so he could park in the gravel parking lot alongside the gray and white Victorian home that welcomed guests. As he climbed out of the car, his phone chimed, but he ignored it and trotted up the wide stairs to the wraparound porch.

Red ribbons spiraled around every porch column. Evergreen boughs hung along the gutters. Sparkling lights in every color framed the windows. He hummed to himself as he glided through the polished walnut door, and Miss Lynette waved at him from the front desk. He waved back and trotted up the carpeted stairs. Once in the soapy-smelling room, he checked the phone and saw it was Bella as he'd assumed. A man with no family didn't receive a lot of personal calls.

With a tired breath, he dropped down onto the double bed and its thick, green comforter. He kicked off his leather loafers. Just in case, he'd brought thick and warm snow boots. He'd be using them sooner than he'd thought if he was lucky.

The phone buzzed again.

"Hello, Bella," he said, easing back against the soft upholstered headboard. He crossed his legs at the ankles.

"Where've you been all day?" echoed a piercing voice. "You said you had an appointment, and you'd call about the meeting tomorrow."

"Yes, I'm just back from the coffee shop," said Pete. Across the room, he waggled his eyebrows in the reflection of the antique mirror that hung over the stout wardrobe. He still looked like a boy from a distance, until the faint crows-feet became clear or one got close enough to see the years in his eyes.

"I hope you found the Darling girl well enough. As far as your job at the little airport, I can meet you there if you like," said Bella. Her voice sounded tinny.

Pete considered it. She was always available, but his personal secretary spent too much time worrying about his life than she did her own. It was supposed to be a work-from-home situation. Wiggling his toes in his socks, he said, "I'm just meeting with the two owners tomorrow to schedule the break down."

"I can run point for you."

"It's going to take me four to six weeks."

"No matter," insisted Bella. "I could do the paperwork here, but it's no problem to join you in Thorpes."

He heard the concern in her voice. She worried when he was on the road, in a foreign town, or around people—not her favorite species—and that he might do something stupid like take a plane up that he had no idea whether or not if it was safe to fly.

"I'll be fine, Bella," he insisted. "Don't worry about me."

She went quiet, then her buzzy voice said with some hesitation, "What about Christmas? You know you hate being alone."

Pete glanced up at his reflection in the mirror again. He wondered what he would look like in a portrait surrounded by children and a dog and most importantly, a beautiful woman with a warm smile. Garland Tate suddenly appeared in his vision, sitting right beside him in the fantasy family picture.

Now there was a problem he'd have to amend. She'd brought up the Darling connection instantly. It was essential to his mission that he remain anonymous. He could only donate the Darling family inheritance to those with a line on the family tree, but it had to remain secret. No one would understand who he was or where he'd come from in case they uncovered the truth. His work at the airport brought in a nice paycheck, but it kept him undercover, too.

"Pete?"

He blinked. "Yes, Bella."

"Call me tomorrow and don't forget to fax me the invoices if I don't make it."

"You got it." He told her goodbye so she could get back to work for her other clients and stop fussing over him. Really, she was indispensable.

He'd known Bella for as long as he could remember. Eons, it seemed. These days, she handled his private business's phone calls, email, invoicing, marketing, and even kept up with his financial records and sent them to a ghostly accountant. He'd never met the man, and that was fine. He seldom did business face-to-face. Everything was computerized these days—his car, his phone, and his bank. Even the cockpits he took apart and examined before putting them back together.

Pete dropped the phone beside him and picked up the television remote control. Since embracing the wintry weather and few swallows of glorious hot chocolate at the Lava Java, he wanted to find a holiday movie to carry on his early feelings of Christmas spirit. It'd be easy to do here in Thorpes.

He glanced around the room as the television powered on, noting the framed forest scenes against the white shiplap walls. His room wasn't as festive as the lobby; it was more subtle. It dampened his mood a little because he loved festive colors, so he turned up the volume on the television and clicked through the channels until he found a cartoon with a singing snowman. This one he knew. Keeping his voice low so his neighbors didn't hear, he turned the captions on and sang along.

CHAPTER TWO

The café closed early on weeknights. Garland wiped down the last café table and headed back to the kitchen. Mariah had already locked up the register, and Doug had cleaned out the coffee machines. He was mopping the back, and Mariah was in her small office staring at receipts with a tired look on her face.

"Hey, I'm done up front." Garland stopped in the office doorway and leaned against the doorframe. "You're not going to be here all night, are you?"

Mariah's head jerked up. "Hm? Oh, no. I have to get home so Darren can get to work."

Garland nodded. "That's awesome Ella has one of you with her at home all day so she doesn't have to go to daycare."

Mariah sat back in her chair. She still wore her dark green apron, and it was splattered with dark stains. "Yes, she's lucky, but Darren never gets to see me."

"Hey," said Garland with a smile, "you're living the dream. Not everyone has the smarts to open their own small business right out of college."

"Yes, I know," said Mariah with a small sigh, "but it's no smashing success even after all these years. I mean, I'm incredibly blessed, but it's so much hard work. I thought I was ready for the sacrifice, you know?" Garland nodded. "But I miss half of Ella's day and never see Darren at all."

Garland smiled like she understood, but she didn't. As far as she could see, family just got in the way of your plans, and second, they let you down. Eventually. "Well," she said trying to think of something cheerful, "soon you'll bring in enough to hire a manager, and you won't have to wear two hats."

"Someday," said Mariah with a faint smile. "It hasn't been a great year, but maybe I'll be able to keep on employees."

"Ha," said Garland. "You got me."

"Yes, for now, until you run off to do your internship. I don't know what I'll do without you. Thank you for staying late again. I can always count on you."

"No worries." Garland waved her off. "I need the extra cash for school anyway, and Doug and I handled it."

"Well, thanks. You were awesome."

Garland remembered her apron and untied the knot behind her back with stiff fingers.

"By the way," said Mariah, "who was the new guy with the supreme cocoa order today?"

"Which one?"

Mariah tilted her head and raised a brow. "Gingerbread Volcano? You know the one."

Garland bit back a smile. "You mean tall, fair, and stalker?"

"Oh, was he? Do tell?" Mariah reached for the teacup on her desk and leaned back again. "He looked alright to me. More than alright."

A funny rolling sensation in her stomach made Garland fold her arms and press them against it. She felt like she'd just climbed off a roller coaster. She took a breath, annoyed at her body's automated responses which paid no attention to her rules. "He was nice but kind of obsessed with his order." She shrugged and tried to look nonchalant. "I don't have time for a Christmas romance."

"He couldn't keep his eyes off you," said Mariah with a grin.

"Yes, I know," said Garland in a wry tone, "creepy. Then he left without finishing his food."

"Maybe he just came to see you."

Garland felt her cheeks warm. "I don't know why. I've never met him before and—" she snapped her fingers, "did you know that he knew my name? I didn't have a name tag on today."

Mariah's smile stiffened. "That is a little weird."

Garland nodded. "He said his name was Pete Darling. Have you ever heard of him before?"

Her friend shook her head, brown eyes lost in thought. "No, but Darling sounds familiar."

"Yes," agreed Garland. "There are Darlings in White Pine Cemetery. My grandfather was a Darling."

"Okay," said Mariah. "That's right. I think a Darling or two played football with my father."

"My uncles, no doubt." Garland didn't elaborate on her opinions of her wild and wacky family.

"Oh, well ask them," said Mariah with concern, "just in case they know who he is."

"I think he's just passing through or something," Garland mumbled back. "I don't ever see my family anyway."

"Yes, I know." Mariah gave her a serious stare. "When's the last time you called your father? Or your sister and brothers? It's almost Christmas."

"Gosh, look at the time," said Garland with a sharp jerk of her head. Over her shoulder, she saw that Doug had finished up and disappeared. It was just like him to clock out without saying goodbye.

"That's right," said Mariah, "ignore the question. You worked and studied all through Thanksgiving, so the least you can do is get in touch with them sometime during the holidays."

"Sure," agreed Garland, "I will." She crossed her fingers behind her back and took two steps backward. "I need to run, or I'm going to be late for class."

"Okay, then, honey. You can uncross your fingers now. Drive safe and watch for ice patches."

"Will do," called Garland. She hurried for the back of the store where her coat and purse were stored. The sloshy rain sounded like it had slowed, and the temperature wasn't low enough to freeze on the roads just yet she hoped.

"See you tomorrow!" She braced herself for a face full of cold rain and swung open the door to dash into the night, forcing work—and Pete Darling—from her mind, because school and finding an internship so she could graduate, along with juggling money, were far more important than coffee, family problems, or mysterious handsome men.

PETE TRIED TO STAY focused during his interviews with the airplane owners. Afterward, he called Bella, faxed her a breakdown of fees, and asked her to invoice them. Work finished, his thoughts returned to his purpose for coming to Thorpes. He strode out of the hangers into the sunshine and climbed into his car.

The high tech sedan careened around the corners of the narrow highway back toward town. On either side of the road, naked trees slouched like gawky teenagers. If it weren't for the sunshine, they'd appear gloomy and gothic.

His stomach grumbled. There was a nice family restaurant on the outskirts of town, but he didn't want to ruin his dinner. He could grab a snack at the café. That was his preference anyway. Checking in on Garland was an obligation, a chance for him to see if he could secretly send some of the inheritance money her way, but he admitted a part of him wanted to see her again. She was a stunning woman, with a girlish face, dark hair, and those legendary Darling blue eyes.

His heart warmed. There had been a friendship with her grandfather, but he hadn't meant to tell Garland so. He'd kept his distance from her mother, but now he'd taken this safety inspection job at Thorpes' regional airport to check in on the next generation. Garland Tate was something else.

The car struggled to know what to do when it came abreast of the Lava Java. Pete turned off the autopilot and eased the car into a vacancy in front of the café. It was between lunch and dinner, but he still felt lucky to find a spot.

He knew from his preliminary research that Garland worked full-time and went to school at night. She lived in a miniature apartment in the back of an old converted home from the forties—the town's heyday—and kept neither cats nor dogs. Her entire life seemed to be nothing but school, school, and waiting tables.

The rest of the Darling family was spread out among the neighborhoods outside of Thorpes. The Darling cousins and Garland's siblings were doing well in their chosen vocations. The oldest sister was married. The younger two boys worked at a car dealership and one was in school. A different school than Garland.

She couldn't get far enough away from her family, he mused. He wondered if they celebrated Thanksgiving together.

He strolled into the shop inhaling the scent of ground coffee beans with pleasure although it wasn't his thing. It smelled comforting, though.

Garland stood at the register, and his heart did an unexpected somersault when he saw her. Her hair was pulled up into a ponytail so he could see the curve of her neck. Her large eyes were framed by dark lashes, and her small mouth had a touch of color. Glancing around at the green boughs and red ribbons around the room with approval, he wondered if she wore plain or peppermint-flavored lip balm.

Her mouth rounded in surprise when she saw him, and it filled him with amusement.

"You're back," she said in a flat tone. He noticed a wary glint in her eyes.

"I am." Her distrust of him was understandable since he'd blurted out her name, but this undisguised suspicion charmed him.

"What will you have?" She stared at the register like she didn't know where else to look. He realized he still wore his work shirt and khakis. He loosened the burgundy tie and scanned the menu overhead.

"I think I'll have a cider today," he said, "and with a shot of salted caramel, if you don't mind." When he looked back at her, she was staring back like she might need to describe him to a criminal sketch artist later.

"Are you going to finish it this time?" She punched in the order on the register without looking up.

"Yes, I had to run yesterday."

"We have takeout containers."

"I'll remember that."

"Will there be anything else?" Her droll tone was meant to put him off, but it was funny. She was interesting—defensive but confident at the same time.

"I'll have a blueberry muffin," he chuckled. Her eyes jerked up to his like that bothered her, too.

The register calculated his total, and he handed her his platinum credit card. Her gaze flicked over it like she was impressed. She ran it and tapped her fingers on the counter while it processed.

"So... new to town?" She tried to sound conversational, but it was forced. Pete knew she hadn't forgotten the name connection the day before.

"Yes and no." He glanced past her like he was watching the latte machine in case she was good at reading faces. "I'm in town for a job at the airport."

"Oh?" The register spat out a snaking receipt, and she tore it off and handed it to him to sign. "My next-door neighbor works at the airport."

Pete smiled. "Small world." He'd thwarted any attempts for her to ask him about his name at least.

She handed him an order number card, and he went to his seat. It was the same table as the day before—the bistro seat in the corner. From there he could watch the townspeople and learn their faces. It was fun to guess their lives and gauge their satisfaction. So many people took what they had for granted—their families, their livelihoods, and even their neighborhoods. It wasn't any of his business, but occasionally he found himself putting someone in their place. He couldn't bear to see people throw it all away. He knew what it was like to have none of those things.

"Darling!" The sound of his surname pricked his heart. He felt a thousand years old when he climbed up from his seat and walked to the counter. Garland held the cup of cider and spun it slowly in small circles like she was waiting on him.

He smiled when she looked up and he saw her eyes had the same wariness in them. "So, Pete Darling, are you a distant cousin or what?"

He urged his racing mind to come up with the right answer.

"Because," the thoughtful woman continued, "Thorpes is full of Darlings. My mother and grandparents are in the town cemetery on the other side of the river."

Peter took the cider from her to keep his hands busy. "I was adopted." He seldom admitted that to anyone.

"Oh, I see. Who were your parents?"

"Darlings," he said with a twinge of pleasure at his obnoxiousness. "My parents are gone, but they're buried in London."

"What are you doing in the states?" Garland was relentless. She may have liked helping people, but she liked interrogating them, too.

"I moved here when I was young. I went to college at Hampton Business School." He took a sip of the hot caramel apple drink and enjoyed the coating of Christmas pleasure it left on his tongue.

"You're a new Englander then."

"I used to be. I live in Florida now."

Garland lifted her chin high in the air. "I see. And you're just in town to do a job and happen to be a Darling."

"That's right."

She crossed her arms and leaned back on the coffee counter behind her. Pete looked over his shoulder to make sure no one stood in line behind him. "And you're a barista in a café. What do you do for fun?"

She watched him carefully. "I go to school full-time."

"All work no play."

"I don't like to play."

"That's a shame. What about the holidays? It's almost Christmas. Shopping, presents, family, magic, romance..."

She scowled. "I don't like holidays. I'm not interested in romance, either."

"I see," he said and gave her a teasing grin. He hoped his cheeks weren't red. They felt warm because at the same time he grinned at her, his brain wondered why he'd thrown the word "romance" into the Christmas activities he'd listed.

"I better get back to work." Garland turned abruptly away.

Pete cleared his throat and tried to look agreeable. "I'm sorry to hear that you don't like Christmas. It's the best time of the year, so maybe I'll have to see if I can change your mind."

Garland sashayed off, her ponytail swinging back and forth. "Good luck with that, Darling!"

CHAPTER THREE

"Tinkerbell tried to kill me." Garland plowed into the café's small back kitchen from the backdoor almost late for her shift.

Mariah burst into laughter. She tried to cover her mouth with the back of her hand since her palms were coated in flour, but it still left powdery smudges on her dark chin. "Who did what?" she called.

Garland swung into the office and dropped her coat and purse beside her boss's things. Her cold ears began to prickle as they thawed in the warmth of the kitchen. She hurried over to the baking counter and picked up a tray of cookies with white chocolate chips waiting to go into one of the ovens.

"We've got fairies in Thorpes now?" joked Mariah. "That's better than the trolls and ogres beating down the doors before we open."

"People like their coffee and muffins early," said Garland. She pulled up a metal stool and plopped herself down on it. Hanging her heels over the bottom rack, she folded her arms. "I had to park across the street because our side is already full, and some skinny fashionista nearly mowed me down with a little black sports car."

"Out of towner?"

"New York plates. She's probably staying at Lynette's B&B on her road trip back to Atlanta or Alabama."

Mariah dusted off her hands with loud clapping sounds. "How do you know she's southern?"

"I don't know." Garland furrowed her brows. "She just looked like a debutante or southern bell—platinum hair, tons of makeup, ruby red lips, lots of jewelry—put together and the opposite of me."

"That's a lot of detail for someone who was almost run over."

"I had a lot of time to examine her in slow motion as her hood ornament came down on me."

"I'm glad you're okay."

"Me, too. Luckily, the road wasn't icy."

"It's supposed to clear up today."

"It's still cold." Garland shivered in her peach knit sweater. She'd worn an undershirt, but the temperature had dropped. Jack Frost was coming.

"Well, happy December." Mariah brushed past her just as the oven timer went off. "At least we get a white Christmas."

"Yes, yes," grumbled Garland. "One more reason to rush and rush before we're snowed in. I'll go plug in the hot water and start grinding beans."

"I think you need a little holiday spirit. There's one more box of decorations that need to go around the windows. Do you mind?"

Garland groaned but walked out to the front. Holiday tunes streamed from the radio. The sun looked ready to rise any moment now. She pushed a few chairs a little further apart and made sure the floor looked spotless. A cardboard box sat on the top of one of the tables nearby. Peering inside, she saw strings of lights that looked like tangled balls of yarn.

"Wonderful." She realized as she said it she felt tired and cranky. Her night classes ran late on Thursdays and left her little time to sleep before the alarm went off a few hours later. Determined to change her attitude, Garland pulled out the first pile of lights and sat down in a chair to unknot them. It'd make the customers happy.

Someone rapped on the locked front door. Garland glanced up at the teapot-shaped clock hanging over the menu board and saw it was one minute past time to open. She tossed the light string to the floor and skipped over to the door. Rhea was there, laptop under her arm and the bottom half of her face hidden behind a fuchsia scarf.

Garland grinned and unlocked the door. "Come in," she said cheerfully. "You're up early. Lots to do today?"

The quiet girl nodded. "I have to work later this afternoon so I need to get my word count in."

Garland nodded at the writer in understanding. "Your roommate was up early?"

"She watches talk shows in the mornings until noon."

"I'm sorry."

Garland patted Rhea's back then walked her up to the counter and let her examine the muffins. After handing her two, she sent the girl to her favorite table and started a breakfast smoothie with cinnamon. Minutes later, she pulled a chair up to the window and began hanging lights around the window frame.

Christmas was unavoidable. The weather seemed colder than usual, which just made the holiday-loving people of Thorpes even more excited about their traditions. A flyer for the annual Yuletide Ball had been taped to the window since early November. There were copies of it posted on the community bulletin board by the front door and in the women's bathroom, too.

Annoying.

Garland hadn't attended the ball since high school. The last year she'd gone for her mother. Mom had wanted to see her baby girl in a taffeta gown with her hair all done up just one more time. Garland had played along because her mother was so sick. The boy she'd gone with had only been a friend, but it'd all been a disaster when he realized he had no chance of getting her under the mistletoe.

Despite the soft ache she felt whenever she thought of her mother, she chuckled as the front door chime sounded. She was too close to finishing the window lighting to stop now. The bulbs flashed red and green and blue against her skin as she tied the end of the string to a corner hook.

"Excuse me!"

A sharp, impatient tone forced Garland to look. She saw a frightfully thin and towering woman in a dark lime skirt suit at the register with her hands on her hips. The stance stretched her jacket open and made a long golden chain swing back and forth across a creamy white blouse. She arched her perfectly manicured brows at Garland. "Coffee?"

The discourteous tone raised Garland's hackles. "In a minute," she said, just crisply enough to not be accused of snapping. She carefully climbed down. Rhea raised an eyebrow at her from across the room when their eyes met then put in her small ear headphones to block them both out.

Garland strode up to the counter, stiffening her back. "Can I help you?"

The woman lifted her chin and studied the menu. Garland forced a polite smile at the stranger. She had a flawless complexion as white and dewy as the first snowfall. She reminded Garland of a pale daffodil, or better yet, a queenly white rose.

"Yes?" Garland prodded, resisting the urge to shuffle her feet. The Amazon ignored her and continued to study her options. Resisting the desire to huff, Garland began at the top: "We have coffee, lattes, teas, cocoa—"

"Shh!" The woman held up a hand like a traffic cop and stopped Garland in her tracks.

She took a small step back so she could stop herself from releasing a New England tirade effused with colorful adjectives. This was the driver of the black sports car who'd almost run her down a half-hour ago.

"When you're ready to order let me know," said Garland in as cool a tone as she could muster. She headed for the kitchen under the pretense of getting a tray of sweets, and added, "By the way, you almost hit me in the crosswalk a few minutes ago."

"Yes," crooned the woman still staring at the menu, "you really should learn to scoot along a little faster."

Garland froze in mid-step. "Excuse me?" A hand automatically went to her waist. Even Mariah's spectacular customer service talents would not tolerate this.

The strapping fairy met her gaze. Her eyes were the palest blue with just a touch of turquoise. They reminded Garland of Pete Darling.

"I'll have a large-sized iced and sugar-free vanilla latte with soy milk and a shot of salted caramel."

Garland opened her mouth while her brain argued over whether or not to tell her to get her uber-urban-ultra-complicated drink order someplace else, like Antarctica. With perfect timing, Mariah burst through the kitchen door carrying a tray of English muffins. The smell of eggs and cheese wafted into the room with her.

"Oh, hello!" she called in her cheerful morning person voice. "You're new." She set the tray down on the counter and reached across it. "I'm Mariah Zobel, the owner of this place."

The customer's mouth snapped into a curt smile that looked practiced. She stuck her arm out in a stiff, slow motion and gave Mariah's outstretched hand two soft pats. "Bella Barrie."

Mariah dropped her hand, and Garland almost snickered at the confused look on her boss's face. "Welcome to Thorpes."

"I'm just passing through, thank the gods." Ms. Barrie gave a pert toss of her head.

Mariah glanced sideways at Garland. "Well, then, I hope you enjoy your visit." She didn't miss a beat. "Garland here will take your order."

Ms. Barrie raised a brow. "I already gave her my order, and I'm waiting. Still."

Mariah's stare froze on the impossibly rude woman. Sensing something in her had just cracked, Garland clapped her hands together to snap everyone out of it. "Yes, great! Let's get that started." She turned back to the latte machine and grabbed a large cup. To her horror, Mariah abandoned her and returned to the kitchen.

Garland scurried over to the mini-fridge for the soy milk, assuming acting fast would have two benefits: the customer couldn't complain, and they'd get her out of here faster.

"So, Garland," said Ms. Barrie from behind her. "How do you like working in this place?"

"I like it just fine. Wait." Garland set the milk on the counter and turned around. An eerie feeling of *déjà vu* washed over her. "How do you know my name?"

It couldn't be a coincidence. Two mind readers in one week?

The woman studied her like she was a stain. She made a flicking motion with her tiny wrist. "Your boss said it. It is Garland, isn't it?"

"Yes," Garland replied. Mariah had called her by name, but there was something too familiar about the way Ms. Barrie said it.

The front doorbell jangled, and two more of the shop's usuals bustled in from the cold. Garland went back to the soy milk and latte machine.

The woman said, "This is a quaint place, but it's not somewhere you want to spend the rest of your life, is it?"

Garland didn't like the disdain. "I like the ambiance," she retorted, "and the people here. I'm fine with it."

"Forever?" The woman snorted. "With a good education and the right connections, you could have an amazing career in New York or Boston."

Garland's heart leapt. How the customer knew that she dreamed of having her own business she didn't know, but the Lava Java was her happy place, a comfortable world she'd lived in since high school. She never let herself think what'd it be like when she had to leave. It would probably feel like losing a family member—like her mother—all over again, but she had no choice if she was going to make it and put some distance between her and the family.

She gave the drink one last squirt of caramel and snapped on the lid. "I'm working on it," she answered.

The woman gave a slow, sarcastic shake of her head. "Ten year plan?"

"Family commitments." How dare the woman insult her career path when she knew nothing about her. Obviously, higher education hadn't been a problem for *her*. Garland pushed the plastic cup across the counter and pounded the price into the register. "That's $8.75."

"My, that's a pricey drink," drawled Monty from his spot in line behind Ms. Barrie. "You must be a fancy lady."

Thorpes' oldest city council member grinned at her, and the woman made a face of horror like he was a monster in a flannel shirt and suspenders. He still wore his wool hat with earflaps, too.

Garland giggled. She tried to catch it, but it slipped out.

Ms. Barrie pursed her lips, threw Garland a silent glare, and then fumbled inside her slim clutch for a credit card. She handed it over and picked up her drink then moved farther away down the counter like they all smelled bad.

When Garland handed her the receipt, she smiled at said, "Enjoy your day in Thorpes. There's another coffee shop up the highway in the next town."

BELLA SURPRISED PETE with an early morning text to tell him she was in town. He couldn't be annoyed with her following him to Thorpes, not with the smell of pancakes drifting upstairs from the dining room below.

He arranged to meet her at the airport hangar later that morning because he knew he'd get greasy. It'd be better to visit Grace first so he didn't have to change. He hadn't seen Grace Darling Hale in years. Garland Tate's great aunt would be about ninety by now.

The Pine Grove Rest Home sat thirty-five minutes away in the pretty countryside, thick with trees that had shed their summer tresses. It was situated on a grassy hill surrounded by a variety of pines—some leggy and tall and others squatty and triangular like Christmas trees. Blue spruces, he guessed, but his botany was not as up to par as his aerospace.

He pulled up the steep drive and around a circular driveway, passing under a large portico to protect visitors from foul weather. Once parked, he hopped out and strode toward the front glass doors, inhaling a deep breath of fresh air. He smiled to himself, happy for the opportunity to see his old friend.

The staff at the front desk wore scrubs but looked friendly. "Peter Darling for Grace Hale," he said, and a young nurse with auburn hair that reminded him of island sunsets, printed out a name tag.

"She's in room 137," she informed him. "Are you family?"

He tried not to fold under her stare. "Why, yes."

"I don't recognize you."

"I haven't visited in a while. Years."

"Okay." The nurse pointed down the hall.

Pete thanked her and ambled down the wide, carpeted hallway that muffled sound and probably cushioned falls. The rooms on either side had their doors ajar, and he heard televisions, radios, and beeping machines. It was more like a resort hospital than a retirement home, but it was the best money could buy within reach of Thorpes. He knew Grace wouldn't be happy away from home, and he'd promised a Darling would never go without if there were anything he could do.

The door to Grace's room was cracked, and he rapped hard so her deaf ears could hear it.

"What?" Her rusted voice sounded welcoming.

He pushed the door open and found her in a recliner oriented towards a good-sized square window. Someone had opened the curtains to allow her to see the view of the trees.

"Hello, Aunt Grace."

The woman stared for a long moment then her watery eyes, once as blue as Garland's, lit up like a candle. "Peter, dear!" She raised her arms in a slow, stiff motion hanging both hands in the air.

Pete strode across the room, leaned down, and embraced her. He felt her worn arms encircle him.

"Oh, you smell like Vermont," she cried, meaning maple syrup. "Did you go to Vermont? To daddy's cabin there?"

"I did," he told her, "and he said for you to hurry home." Pete knew there was no use telling her the family cabin on her husband's side of the family was never in Vermont. He pulled a small plastic chair away from the wall and sat down in it across from her.

Grace clapped her hands together. "I'm going to swim in the lake," she beamed, "like we used to do. Do you remember Peter?"

"Yes, Grace. I remember."

"There were mermaids! I used to be a mermaid."

He smiled at her confused mind. She'd always been a strong woman, much like her niece, but age had taken its toll. The poor darling. She'd lost a brother and a husband.

"I like my new house," she said, chattering on like a little gray squirrel that was happy to see him. "Do you?"

Pete looked around the room. The walls held watercolor paintings signed in her name and there were also rough sketches. The most recent art therapy looked like colored pencil-embellished stick figures and flowers.

"I love your new house." There was no point in telling her she'd lived here for over ten years. "How are you, Aunt Grace? Are they kind to you? Do they feed you well?"

"Oh, yes," said Grace, "we have pancakes every day."

Pete searched her eyes. She smiled back and pointed a withered finger at him. "You bought this house for me, didn't you?"

"Um, yes," he said in a low voice. "I bought your house for you so you'd be safe."

"Until I can fly away." She gazed at him lovingly. It was almost like having a mother—something he'd never known. Although he'd only met her once when she was young and vibrant, she was a Darling, and he loved and respected her.

"You deserved the money," he told her. "You worked hard, raised a family, and took care of your husband until he... flew away," Pete stammered. "I know you wanted to live with Martha Ann, but she can't handle an independent woman like you."

Pete knew that Grace's neighbor who had cared for her for years wouldn't be able to take care of a woman with dementia.

"I love my house," she told him and clapped her hands together again. "I'm glad you stayed to grow up. Now, where's my pancakes?"

Pete laughed and stood up. "Haven't you had your breakfast? Should I go find you some pancakes?"

Grace gasped with delight. "Yes," she cried. "Yes!" A red-beaded bracelet swung around her bony wrist in time with her childish excitement.

"You stay right there." He pulled on the door handle to check the hall for someone to help rather than hitting the nurse call button. To his surprise, Garland stood in the doorway. She looked frozen, about to stalk in, with her hair out of its usual ponytail and her fair cheeks blazing with a red flush.

"Uh... hey!" His enthusiasm hit the floor with a dread-filled thud. What was she doing here? By the lightning in her eyes, he was certain invisible steam was shooting out of her ears.

"What are *you* doing with my aunt?" Her words came out sharp and staccato.

Pete noticed a bulky-looking orderly watching from a few doors down. He swallowed. He wasn't in the mood to confront a giant. He held his hands out and gave Garland what he hoped was a calming smile.

"I'm a Darling," he said. "I came to talk family history. How did you know?"

"Family history?" Garland glared. "The front desk called me because they didn't recognize you, and Grace never had children, so don't tell me now that you're her long lost son."

Pete tried not to let her see his chest deflate. So much for that one. "I happened to look through an old phone book at the B&B and saw her name in there. So many Darlings," he finished with a grin.

"Not that many." Garland folded her arms and stared at him with blazing azure eyes.

"Peter! Where are my pancakes?"

Pete glanced over his shoulder to make sure Grace still sat in her chair. He didn't want her to trip and fall. "I'll have them in thirty seconds, Grace. Can you count down for me?"

She started singing her ABC's, and Garland pushed past him into the room.

"Hi, Aunt Grace," she crooned. She walked over and dropped into Pete's chair. "How are you? I haven't seen you since last Sunday. Do you remember Sunday?"

Grace tilted her head. "We go to church together," she said in an obedient tone.

"Yes, we do," said Garland in a reassuring voice. She threw Pete a warning look. "I see Mr. Darling is visiting you today. Are you having a nice time?"

Grace looked over at Pete who stood by the bed, and he raised his arm in a little wave. "He's my cousin," she announced. She looked at him fondly. "We're going swimming tomorrow."

He gave her a bow.

Garland huffed. "No, Aunt Grace, you can't go swimming tomorrow. It's too cold outside. You wait here, and I'll check on your breakfast." Her great aunt frowned. Garland patted Grace's shoulder then inserted herself between the recliner and the bed to block Pete's view.

"She doesn't even know who I am, and you expect her to give you the family history? You're a complete stranger."

Peter grimaced. She had no idea how cutting her words were even if they were true. "I just wanted to meet another family member from across the pond."

"There's no one left," Garland hissed in a low tone. "The only Darlings around here are my sister and two brothers, and we're not even Darlings, we're Tates."

He grit his teeth to hide his impatience. "Grace and her brother were Darlings, their father was a Darling, and so are you."

"Yes, and they're all gone. Seriously, Pete, what do you want? At most, we're distant cousins. So we share the same last name on a pie chart, so what?"

He snorted. "It's called a family tree."

"So?" She glared, and he realized he'd blown it. She thought he was nuts, or worse, dangerous. All he'd wanted to do was check on Grace, get a glimpse of this Garland Tate working so hard to make it on her own, and make sure the family had what they needed.

"So is your aunt here just an obligation?" He didn't keep the sadness out of his tone. "You really don't have any use for family ties, do you?"

Garland stared, for once speechless. Grace started singing *Jingle Bells*.

"Just add that to my list," Garland whispered.

"Oh, that's right. No Christmas, no romance, and no family. Wow," he said, unable to withhold the sarcasm, "you're some Darling. A strong, ambitious, no-nonsense—"

"Stop it, Pete."

"—independent," he continued, "do-it-all-on-your-own, don't need anyone—"

"I mean it," she hissed. "I have big plans, and I'm not ashamed of it." Her blue eyes looked like icicles on fire.

"What happened?" Pete said in a low tone. He saw her swallow and knew he'd hit a nerve.

"It's none of your business." Her eyes became glossy like somewhere deep in her heart she was fighting back tears.

"Leave. Now," Garland said in a strangled voice. "I'm her advocate and legal guardian, and I want you to leave before you upset her."

Grace was on the second verse and clapping her hands.

"Fine," he said, digging deep for patience. "I'm sorry if I invaded your personal space. I just thought I'd have a nice visit with a distant relative."

"If you want to have relatives, go back to England."

Garland's words pierced through his emotional armor. "I don't have any relatives left in England," he retorted. "I don't have family anywhere." He stalked out of the room, temper in the stratosphere, throwing glares at the orderly waiting outside.

"Are you leaving now?" The man built like an Indian chief had a stern tone.

Pete threw him a challenging look. He might have been less muscled, but he was light on his feet and had never lost a fight. Well, he admitted as the cool December air calmed his temper and slowed his pulse, he'd just lost this one. He wouldn't be able to check on Grace again for a while, and it left a sour taste in his mouth.

He stomped out of the facility's front doors. Garland's siblings were doing okay. He hadn't made a nuisance of himself checking in on their affairs, so why did he keep looking for reasons to see her again and again? Her tuition could be paid anonymously if it was something she needed, but she seemed to have a handle on things and probably wouldn't want it.

Pete exhaled and touched the car's door handle which automatically opened the car door. The job at the hanger could keep him out of her path if he wanted to avoid her. It wasn't like she hung out at the B&B. He slid into the velvet-soft seats and stared at the technologically advanced monitor that did all the thinking for him.

There were less than five hundred of these cars on the roads, and they weren't cheap. He'd bet the blued-eyed, sultry Darling with big dreams would be impressed with his silly toy. He glanced back toward the rest home. Poor Garland. She had it all wrong. Being successful in the eyes of the world didn't mean you could escape your past or where you came from. She belonged in Thorpes. It needed her.

CHAPTER FOUR

Garland parked her beat-up car beside the dilapidated porch entrance to her apartment and unlocked the door with stiff fingers. Once inside her small apartment, she bolted the door, checked the windows, and walked through the studio apartment to make sure everything looked secure. Not that there was any crime in Thorpes, but something about her day—no, her week—had left her rattled.

The arms of the clock crept toward midnight. She'd stayed after her late night business class to study with a partner and sketch out an idea for the semester group project. Just one more semester working an internship, and she'd have her dual degree. It'd taken long enough.

She plodded into the bathroom to wash up for bed. In the mirror, she searched for bags under her eyes, but she looked fine despite her fatigue. She'd missed a couple hours of work running down to the rest home to make sure Aunt Grace wasn't entertaining lawyers or con men.

Pete Darling wasn't a lawyer as far as she could tell. Con man? She wasn't sure. She looked down and turned on the faucet. She knew her cheeks flushed whenever she thought of him. It irritated her. She'd dated on and off since high school, but nothing serious. Men seemed put off by her ambitions, and it wasn't fair. The only way to have distance from her family was out of Thorpes, and the only way to get out of Thorpes was with hard work and a good degree.

She let out a long breath and tried to push Pete Darling from her mind. Settling meant growing up alone, starting college late in life, losing your family, and almost missing out on your dreams. The last thing she wanted to do was dream about some distracting stranger. He already haunted her thoughts since he'd crept into her café. Really, the man was nothing but trouble.

Saturday morning arrived like a warm, cozy blanket. She wished she had a fireplace. The upstairs apartment did. Considering the benefits of having a natural heat source on Thorpes' chilly winter mornings, Garland made a hot breakfast before heading over to the community center for her volunteer hours. Mariah asked all employees to help with service projects to represent the coffee shop, and Garland liked them for her resume. It looked good on internship applications.

She threw on jeans and a thick sweatshirt with the Lava Java logo embroidered across the front and braided her hair since she had the time. There were candy cane earrings in her jewelry box Mariah had given her last year in hopes of passing on some Christmas spirit. Her fingers hovered over them before choosing the white pearl studs that had belonged to her mother. Her sister, Joy, had coveted them, but Joy had received the necklace since she was oldest, not that anyone would have known it when Mom got sick. The only one who stayed at her side was Garland.

Shoving back the painful memories, she popped the earrings in, checked her makeup in the mirror, and grinned at her bright lipstick. She never had time to go the extra mile during the week and since she felt like a sweatshirt today, it didn't hurt to polish herself up in other areas.

Garland picked up her backpack-style purse and trotted out to the car. The sun wasn't shining today and any later potential didn't look good. Frozen gravel crunched under her feet like dry bones. She shivered. Hopefully, the community center's gym would be warm for those who showed up to pack snacks and dry goods for children in need of extra nutrition during the Christmas break.

The drive over took less than ten minutes, hardly enough time for the car's heat to warm up. She parked in the front, glanced down the street, and saw little action at the park where they'd set up a temporary ice rink. Too early.

She hurried into the center. Busy volunteers darted back and forth across the hallway between a storage closet and the events room.

Garland answered greetings from acquaintances, signed in at the welcome table, and scurried over to her assigned spot at a long table to commandeer dry pasta in the bucket brigade. She felt her heart lift as early-morning fatigue slipped away. She was happy on the inside, the same way she felt when she drove into town after being gone a few days. There was something homey and welcoming about her life in Thorpes, but there was nothing here for her. She'd miss it when she left.

Fifteen minutes into packing spaghetti noodles into containers and passing them left, she felt a light tap on her shoulder. She looked up into the teal gaze of Pete Darling.

"Long time no see," he said with cheerfulness.

She felt her mouth drop open in astonishment. He laughed. "I had no idea you'd be here, I promise."

He held his hands up in surrender and motioned back with his chin. "See? Miss Lynette rounded up everyone at the Blackberry Inn to volunteer for a good cause. I rode over with her."

Garland glanced back at the row of familiar and not-so-familiar faces. "Oh," she muttered, a strange swish of relief sweeping through her chest. "If this town were any bigger, I'd take out a restraining order I hope you know."

"Please don't do that. I'd miss my cocoa and cider."

She exhaled loud enough for everyone to hear.

"So," he said, picking up a box and handing it to her, "you don't work on Saturdays?"

She shook her head. "It's my day off today. I need time to study."

"Then it's nice of you to spend a few hours here."

Garland noticed Pete had tried to dress casually. There were no expensive trousers or dress shirts. His jeans looked new and trendy though, and his sweater too Italian to have been purchased in Thorpes. Its fawn-colored shade made him look tanned. Ruby highlights in his hair gleamed under the lights.

Realizing she was studying him, she put the box of food dangling in her hand into the next box and passed it off to the woman beside her packing boxes of rice. "I like to volunteer once a month," she said, realizing she'd dropped the ball. "It's good for Lava Java, and I can list it on my resume."

"Are you sure you don't do it because you like helping people?"

Garland blinked. "Sure."

Pete handed her a new empty box so she could fill it. "I think you like people more than you let on."

"Maybe."

"Uh-huh. You love serving coffee at the Lava Java. I see the way you smile at the old-timers that come in. And you always make time to talk to people who come in alone, like the Rhea girl who's always there, clicking away on her laptop.

Garland shrugged. "I've lived here all my life, it's not a big deal."

"I think it is. Lots of people grow up and stay in the same town and never bother to get to know anyone outside their circles. You seem to know everyone."

Garland thought about the people she met at the café. It didn't take long for new move-ins to find it. She had old friends from high school. Church was always a place of warmth and security. "I guess you're right," she admitted, "but I like going places and meeting new people, too, who aren't from around here."

Pete chuckled. "I wouldn't have known it considering your reaction when you met me."

"You just surprised me is all," Garland explained. "The Darling name threw me off."

"Yes, I can see that."

She narrowed her eyes. "So what do you do at the airport? You aren't working today?"

"Later, actually. I'm a freelance safety inspector. I have my own business examining private planes for their owners to make sure they're safe and ready to fly."

"Like with the FAA?"

"No, not like that. I'm not with the government." Together, they began to pack and pass the donation boxes faster. "Government inspectors do commercial planes. Inspections for experimental craft, or just personal, hobby-type planes aren't required. That's where I come in. A lot of pilots want to make sure their new purchase is safe or if something's been repaired, that it was done right."

Garland glanced over at his attire. "So, you're a glorified mechanic. It must be a lucrative career."

"I guess. I love to fly, and I don't get to do it often, but this is one way I can have income and do both." He shrugged. "It works."

"Mm," she grunted. "It more than works I'd say, by your watch and the car you drive. Don't think I don't notice all the ladies staring whenever you walk into a room."

He grinned. "The car is just for fun. Most of my income is inherited." He hesitated then said brusquely, "I just have some family money, I mean."

"Oh," said Garland. Something pricked the back of her mind, and she remembered an odd family story. "My grandfather used to tell us the family was quite wealthy during the Industrial Revolution. His father's mother, Wendy Darling Pruitt, gave all of the money away to an orphanage—or an orphan—after she died."

Garland looked up at Pete and grinned. "Maybe your side stole it." His face seemed to pale. She burst into laughter and nudged him with her hip. "I'm joking. Seriously. If you're a cousin than surely you know my side of the family is nowhere near rich, not to mention a little crackers."

He pressed his lips together. "Those are the best kind to have."

She thought of her family and how broken it all felt. "Not for me," she mumbled. "I prefer people who step up instead of losing their marbles." She saw him watching her with a look of mingled amusement and concern. "It's a long story." Not one she wanted to talk about.

A whistle blew, and they both jumped. "Wow, that went fast." She smiled at him.

"Doing things for others usually does." Pete reached out and took her by the hand. "Come on, let's go over to the snack table and get something to eat before you head off to your study session."

Garland's fingers prickled where he touched her. It turned into a tingly burn that crept up her arm. Surprised, she caught herself smiling as she strolled with him over to a small concession table.

They picked out cheese crackers, sliced oranges, and bananas, and she pointed to a row of chairs against the wall. "Let's sit there."

Around the room, directors sent sealed boxes through the side door and out to waiting vans. Volunteers stood in small circles, talking and laughing with one another.

"You have a nice community." Pete slid down beside her after she took a seat, and she felt the magnetic warmth of his closeness as his leg brushed up against hers. It made her heart do a pirouette—like a drunk ballerina.

Garland blinked and gave her head a sharp shake to clear it. "Yes, Thorpes is a warm and friendly place, if anything. They go a little overboard when it comes to the holidays, but I try to overlook it."

Pete tossed a small square cracker into his mouth with practiced skill. "It's magical, and believe me, I know magic when I see it. So why do you act like you want to leave so badly if you like it here so much?"

Garland felt her heart sink. The truth hurt. She fiddled with an orange slice letting the juice make her fingers sticky as she turned it over in her hand. "I always wanted to have my own business, like a boutique or even a bookstore, where I can run things the way I like and make good money so I don't need anything from anyone."

"But away from here?" Pete munched his cracker and swallowed. "Most small businesses don't make a whole lot of money no matter where they're located."

"I will." Garland felt stubborn pride rise in her chest. "I'm pretty good at making a success of anything I set my mind to, and the reality is, I don't want to stay. There's not much keeping me here."

"You just said everything was wonderful in Thorpes."

Garland stared across the gym. "Not my family."

"What's wrong with them?"

She shrugged. "We're just not close," she explained when she realized he was determined to hear something. "My mother died when I was in high school, and I guess, that was that. We sort of... crumbled apart."

"So," Pete said, "you think going somewhere else and making lots of money will make you feel better?" His tone irritated her.

"It's not that," Garland retorted as his words pierced her chest. "We never had much. My father taught at the high school and didn't make much. He was super old-fashioned and insisted that my mother not work. Then when my grandfather died there wasn't even enough money to pay for the funeral. Luckily, some anonymous benefactor took care of it—probably our church congregation. It was embarrassing."

"Maybe they just wanted to be kind. It doesn't mean there was judgment."

Garland glanced over at Pete's expensive-looking watch. "No offense, but I don't think you can understand." He opened his mouth to say something then closed it and looked away.

"My mother found out she had breast cancer my sophomore year of high school. By the time I graduated, the insurance ran out. We took care of her the best we could—or I did, because no one else could deal with it—but once again, someone had to secretly step in and pay off our bills so we didn't lose the house."

She looked Pete in the eye to make sure she had his attention. "It's hard depending on other people and falling short. My mother depended on me, and she died. That's why I'm so..."

"Loyal?" She looked at him in surprise, and he grinned. "You've worked for Mariah for years, and I bet you've had better job opportunities. It's admirable, even as you're killing yourself in night school."

"Ha," grumbled Garland. "I had to take care of my mother instead of starting college. That's why I'm so behind, but you know now why I'm doing it. I'm going to make something of myself and make my mother proud. I'm going to get out of here and come back someday and buy out other people's problems, kind of like paying forward."

"Again, admirable," said Pete. "Believe it or not, I completely understand that."

Garland sniffed. Her tirade had caused her throat to tighten up. "Well, I bet you don't understand what it feels like taking forever to reach your goals. If my mother hadn't gotten sick..."

"You wouldn't have had to wait so long to start college," he finished. "Oh, yes," he nodded, although he disagreed. "I understand exactly what that's like to have to wait for what you want."

PETE FELT LIKE HE WAS floating when he drove out to the airport. Even the overcast sky didn't bother him. He hadn't expected to see Garland at the community center. Her attitude toward him had softened, and it filled him with a strange happiness. He tapped his index finger on the steering wheel, enjoying the opportunity to drive his own car rather than letting it drive him.

His heart skipped along in his chest like a bubbling brook. They weren't really related—quite distantly so on paper and only through adoption. How was it she could be so different and he feel so connected?

In the back of his mind, something whispered that he couldn't let himself fall for a Darling. His job for the old estate was to distribute the family money anonymously since Wendy Darling's beneficiaries were conned of their rightful inheritance. He'd made it his duty in life to see that he spread the wealth around the family tree as much as he could, but if he told anyone or explained where the money came from, it would all be divvied out after the majority went to the lawyers and banks, and he would be out. Bella kept tabs on him for more than one reason. No one would believe his real story.

Pete pulled into the airport office's parking lot and an accidental groan escaped. Bella's black sports car gleamed from its lone parking space far away from anything else so it didn't get dented or scratched. Sighing, he climbed out of the car. The woman was adamant they work together in person whenever she could make it happen. He waved at an old fellow at the front desk and strode back to the hanger where his client's newly-crafted twin-engine Cessna was stored.

Bella sat in a camp chair with a wrinkled nose although her pants suit looked as immaculate as her lovely complexion. "It's about time." She shuffled a stack of papers in her delicate hands.

He crossed the room as he pulled a work jumpsuit out of his travel tote. "I told you I wouldn't be in until after lunch. We had a service project at the community center."

Bella raised an eyebrow. "We? You know you don't actually live in Thorpes. You're a guest here, and the Blackberry Inn and everyone else will forget about you as soon as you're gone."

"Thanks," he muttered.

"Don't worry, I won't," she promised him.

Even though it was meant to be comforting, Pete felt exasperated. "I know you won't, Bella. I can't run this business without you."

"That's not what I meant," she huffed.

"You're appreciated," he relented. She was a driven woman now, but she still had an insatiable need to be admired and worshiped more than was usual in his experience. Clothes protected, he leaned over her shoulder to examine the invoice.

"Did the payment already go through?"

"Of course it did." Bella tilted her head so her hair brushed his cheek. "I sent it twice and called him yesterday."

Pete laughed. "The poor guy. I'm barely a third of the way done on this plane, and you're hounding him for the payment."

"You're one of the few in the country, and you're the best. He's lucky he didn't have to wait until next summer since you're so booked ahead."

Pete headed for the cockpit of the plane. The engine check was complete. "His builder did a good job. This one is in prime condition."

"Good to know." Across the hanger, Bella bobbed her crossed leg up and down. Her spike heel looked like a dangerous weapon. "There's a French restaurant an hour east of here—more to our taste. I made reservations for eight o'clock."

"Sounds good," Pete mumbled. He'd prefer something local, like trying out the pizza place north of city hall, but as usual, she'd already gone to the trouble. Sometimes he felt torn between her loyalty and her hunger for something more from him, but it could never be.

"So," he mused. He glanced over and found her watching him with an intense stare. "How long do you plan to hang around? I appreciate you coming out to meet the owners with me, but I know you aren't fond of the oil and grease, not to mention town.

"Such simple people," she complained. "The nail salon is a dungeon. It's medieval."

He laughed from the empty cockpit, and it echoed off the hanger ceiling.

"I'm staying to make sure you don't get yourself into trouble."

Pete looked sideways across the room then back at the wires in his hands. "You don't always show up to do that."

"Well, it's this Tate thing. You already checked out the siblings last year. Why didn't you just hire a private investigator like you usually do?"

He shrugged. "There's something about New England."

"It reminds you of home, that's what it is," said Bella with a frown.

"London? Maybe. That was so long ago though."

"Well, it never snows in L.A., and I like it."

"It never snows in Florida either."

She made a gagging noise. "I tried that. It's too humid, and the people are so..."

"Friendly?"

Bella huffed, and he looked up from his work. She lifted her shoulders in acknowledgment. "Southerners," she said in a horrible drawl of imitation.

"What about New Englanders?"

"Traitors and rebels." She threw on her British accent.

He laughed again. "Independent," he corrected her. "Garland surely is."

"Hmph! Ridiculous name," snapped Bella.

"It's a Christmas thing. Her sister's name is Joy. The younger brother's name is Nicholas."

"Oh for pity's sake!"

Pete set down his tools and climbed out of the open cockpit. "I think it's fun. Her parents obviously loved this time of year. I don't know why she doesn't."

"Holidays are a waste of good health and good money," disagreed Bella. Her crossed leg stopped its impatient bouncing.

"You sound like Garland."

In a tight voice, Bella said, "You already checked on her and the aunt. I don't know why you insist on going into town so often."

Pete walked across the concrete floor to the mini-fridge against the wall. "I'm staying in town," he said trying to sound patient. "The inn's a street south of city hall and just a block away from the park."

"I know. I've seen it. It's practically smothered in light bulbs. So garish."

He chuckled and said, "Says the woman from L.A."

"That's different," she snapped, "and so is this place. You best go straight back to Florida when you're done here." Her voice swam with warning.

"Why?" He shrugged like it didn't matter, but he really wanted to know. Did she suspect what he did? When he gave Bella a questioning stare she looked away and said nothing. He smacked his lips, set the water bottle on the table beside her, and walked back to the plane.

Thorpes was a rather comfortable place. It felt... homey to him. Besides, the distant relative on the family tree he was checking up on might need some financial help if she didn't find an internship. Worse, he admitted to himself, he didn't like the idea of going away without spending more time with her.

CHAPTER FIVE

Pete ambled into the Lava Java about an hour after the lunchtime rush, and Garland automatically reached for the cocoa powder. To her dismay, her heart did a barrel roll at the sight of him.

"Good afternoon. Is it scary that I'm starting to think of you as a local?" She braced herself before meeting his eyes. All weekend she had to force herself to stop thinking she could have feelings for this complete stranger. She hoped it explained her breathlessness. Maybe he'd think she was busy although the big crowd had thinned out.

"You're making my drink already."

Garland stopped in midair, about to ring up his purchase although she still had whipped cream and garnishes to add. "Did you want something else?"

He grinned at her. "No, what you have is fine. It's drizzly again today. I'm running out of sweaters."

"You don't have a lot of sweaters in... Florida?"

"Miami," he said.

"That's right. To be honest, I figured you for a New Yorker or something."

"I travel so much I shouldn't really lay claim to Florida, to be honest."

"Right." Garland noted he wore blue jeans again instead of fancy slacks and that there were faint oil stains on the corners of his fingernails. He noticed her studying him and smiled.

She blinked and looked back at the register. After running his card he murmured, "Thank you," and their eyes met. Her cheeks flushed, and she turned back in mortification to garnish his drink. She imagined his gaze on the back of her neck, and it made her feel even warmer, almost hot.

"Here," she mumbled, passing the mug over to him.

"You look nice today," he said out of the blue.

She glanced down at her long-sleeved blouse and black slacks. "I have a presentation—

school project."

He accepted the hot cup. "The semester must almost be over?"

"Yes. Finally."

"That'll give you some free time during Christmas."

She stared at him. "Free time means I'm standing still."

He chuckled and lifted the cup in a salute. "Good luck with final exams."

Garland let herself smile at him again as her heart filled with gratitude. It was nice to know someone understood how busy she was. "Thanks."

When Mariah came back from her break, she took over the counter, and Garland went back to the kitchen for a dish towel and spray bottle. Doug had already swept the floors after the noon-time rush. She was halfway across the room and working her way down the middle row when Pete looked up from his newspaper.

"Do you need any help?"

She swiped a crumb trail off of a table surface. "You don't work here."

"I might as well. I'm here just about every day."

Garland straightened and stretched. "Don't they have coffee at the B&B?"

He looked amused. "I'm not much of a coffee drinker."

"That's right." She crossed the space between them and leaned back on the table next to his. "You have a sweet tooth, don't you?"

"Guilty." His mouth stretched into a wide smile.

"I guess you get into Halloween, too?"

Pete looked off toward the door like he was thinking. "Nope," he said, "it's not the same. The candy's not homemade, and people don't get together like they do for Christmas."

She almost shook her head in disgust. "You mean like family get-togethers?"

He nodded. She remembered his outburst about not having any family and felt sorry for him. At least she knew what a family was supposed to be like—she'd had good times when she was little. Those were the years before Mom got sick.

"I'm sorry you don't have much family." She watched him, wondering if he'd tell her more. Instead, his eyes clouded over. "Thanks." They watched each other for a few seconds then he added, "I saw they have an ice rink set up at the park."

"They do every year."

"There's a nice big Christmas tree, too."

She sniffed. "We have lots of Christmas tree farms around here, plus the cold weather. I think the city council fancies Thorpes as exciting a place to ice skate as Rockefeller Center in New York."

Instead of laughing, Pete said, "I think it's far more charming."

"Oh, do you skate?" Garland couldn't imagine it. He was too suave to risk falling onto his behind on the ice.

"Actually," he admitted, "I've never ice skated in my life. I think I'd be pretty awesome."

Garland burst out laughing. "If you say so yourself!"

"Well, I fly, and I ski. Then there's hang gliding and parasailing. Why not?"

"That's completely different. What about scuba diving?"

He frowned. "Water sports are not my thing."

"And you live in Miami?" Garland gave him a teasing grin, and he shrugged.

"I prefer staying above sea level, thank you very much."

She couldn't stop smiling. The thought that he felt afraid of something as silly as the ocean made him seem more human. "Not a shark guy, huh?"

"No, or alligators or crocodiles, either."

"Okay." Garland pursed her lips. "So you're not a reptile man. What about deer and moose and foxes?"

"I can handle them."

"Skunks? Coyotes?"

"They don't bother me." Pete sat back in his chair and grinned. "I'm fearless when it comes to mammals."

"Uh-huh." She couldn't help teasing. He seemed to be smitten with Thorpes. "Well," she said with a shrug, "it's a good thing you like cold weather. You'll find all of that here and more."

He glanced up at her—she could have sworn through his lashes. Then she realized Mariah was watching from the counter and said, "I better get back to work."

Pete set the newspaper down flat on the table. "Hey Garland," he said before she could step away, "would you go ice skating with me?"

Garland's feet felt bolted to the floor. Her heart skipped a beat and then picked back up so loud she was sure Pete could hear it. "Um, sure," she said her brain too surprised to come up with another reply.

"Great." He gave her a faint smile. "How about next Monday night? Do you have a class?"

"Tuesday and Thursday are my late classes," she admitted, "but I'll be done by seven on Wednesday night." She gave him an apologetic grimace. "It's kind of late."

"That's not a problem."

There was no way she was going to get out of it. He really wanted to ice skate. "Okay, then. I'll meet you there a little after seven."

"Sounds great." Pete stood up, and she took a step back. "We can grab something to eat afterward at Magici Pizza."

Garland sucked in a nervous breath. "Sure, that sounds fine." She forced a smile on her face and dashed back to the kitchen. Doug looked up from the sink in surprise. "I'm fine," she said.

She darted to the bathroom like she needed to use it. Instead, she stared at herself in the mirror for a long minute than washed her hands and reapplied her lip balm. When she came out, Mariah stood outside the door with her arms crossed and her brows raised.

"And?"

Garland looked around, desperate to do anything besides spill her guts—or her heart. "Where's Doug?"

"I sent him to mind the register. What was that? You practically broke the sound barrier running back here."

Garland's chest crumpled, and she let her shoulders droop. "He asked me out."

"Pete?" Mariah grinned and dropped her mouth open at the same time.

"Stop it." Garland stalked over to examine the order tickets clipped over the pass-through window.

Her boss followed her, but at least she'd lowered her voice. "What'd you say?"

"I didn't have time to think it through."

"Tell me you did not turn that gorgeous airplane pilot down." Mariah frowned at her.

Garland stood on her tiptoes and peered through the window and saw that Pete was gone. She sighed with relief. "No," she said, looking back at Mariah and hoping her cheeks didn't blush again. "I said 'yes' without even considering the consequences, and by the way, he's not a pilot, he does safety inspections."

Mariah grinned. "Then he's probably safe."

"I doubt it."

"Oh, babe. You do not have to keep living your life like someone's going to chain you down."

Garland sniffed. She didn't need to explain why she had to be successful and do it on her own.

Mariah's eyes filled with tenderness. "Don't assume anyone you fall in love with is going to let you down or not be there for you if something were to happen."

Garland's throat tightened. The little girl in her wanted to burst into tears, but she took over. "It's fine, Mariah," she said in a firm tone. "It's just a little ice skating."

Mariah clapped her hands, winked, then skipped to her office humming to herself. Garland looked around for something to do besides return to the front and deal with customers again. The sink was sagging with dishes. Feeling sorry for Doug, she walked over to finish up his chores.

IT WAS A NIPPY LATE evening, and Thorpes looked like a winter wonderland even without its first heavy snowfall. Twinkling lights crisscrossed Main and Becker streets and made the park look like it was surrounded by a magical village. The lampposts were swagged in silver garland with evergreen wreaths and scarlet bows, and the brick corner wall of the bakery was decorated with a Christmas scene of three wise men.

Pete parked across the street beside the bakery and jogged over the crosswalk to the park's northwest corner. All of the trees in the park were wrapped in lights from trunks to treetops that shimmered in soft shades of blues and creams.

He zipped his jacket up and shivered. The only sweater he'd bought, his brown cashmere pullover, was warm enough for fall, but the temperature had dropped like a sandbag this afternoon. It would have been the perfect day to have a warm drink at the Lava Java, but he'd just seen Garland a few days before and didn't want to make her feel uncomfortable.

His mouth twitched as he recalled the red rash that broke out around her neck and spread to her jawline when he'd asked her to go skating. He hadn't meant to make it sound like a date, but that's what it was, and he knew it. By the time he'd finished tossing and turning all night and dragged himself over to the hanger the next morning, he realized that's what he wanted it to be.

There was no denying it anymore. He was immensely attracted to Garland—as a woman and as a friend. It had nothing to do with the Darling family or money. She was special—soft in the heart but a little scraped up on the outside—kind of like him once upon a time. He loved her ambition and how hard she worked, and he knew that she really cared about people.

Her familiar silhouette at the gate to the rink caught his attention. Picnic tables were lined up in neat rows for people to sit on and remove their shoes or drink cocoa. Gleaming light bulbs dangled from wires strung from tree to tree.

She stood on her toes when she spotted him and waved. He waved back. She wore a gray knit cap pulled over her head, and her hair was down. It shined under the lights.

"Wow," he said when he reached her. He meant her fresh-faced beauty, but he leaned over the fence to examine the ice skating rink like he meant that instead. It was oval-shaped and built around a large stationary gazebo in the middle.

"I love all these lights," admitted Garland. Her breath made frosty wisps in the air with each word.

"The gazebo looks amazing. I like all of the red and green decorations around it."

"Plus they set up a tree in the center." Garland pointed. "All of the ornaments are birds and nests. It's beautiful."

"I'll have to take a closer look," said Pete. It was just like they'd spoken a few hours ago instead of a couple days. He wondered if she'd been looking forward to tonight as much as he had.

"I haven't done this since before my mother died." Her eyes looked bright and her face rosy, but he saw a shimmer of regret. She blinked and tossed her head with a renewed smile. "Let's go!"

He laughed at her excitement and took her hand, wishing she didn't have on gloves. They traipsed up to the outdoor booth and ordered skates, and Pete reached for his wallet before she could pull something out of her pocket.

"Oh, I have mine," she said breathlessly.

"No, please," he pleaded. "I've never done this, and I dragged you out here, so let me cover this."

Her mouth twisted into a small grimace, but she relented. "Okay, but I'll get the pizza later."

He glanced at her with an amused smile. "We'll split it."

She sighed.

"I really don't mind. Let me be a gentleman, please."

Garland pursed her lips at him, but a dimple nicked her cheek. "Thank you," she said, "it's appreciated." Her humility astonished him.

"I thought I'd have to arm wrestle you over paying," he admitted, "but I like to do it, and I can afford it."

"So can I," she said with a stubborn grin. She took the skates the cashier handed over and started for an empty bench. Pete followed her from behind, admiring her straight silky locks and the trim fit of her dark jeans.

"I like your puffy jacket," he joked, and she giggled. After lacing up, they tottered over to the rink entrance with snickers, and Garland went first. She wobbled a little as she crossed onto the ice but then she caught her balance with outstretched arms and did a small, sturdy circle.

"Come on," she called as other skaters passed by. Christmas songs echoed over loud speakers, and the cold air amplified it over the laughter of everyone enjoying the night.

Pete swallowed, and he stepped out onto the ice. It was like riding a bike, even though he'd never tried skating before. He floated across the rink, stiffened his ankles and knees, and bumped hard into the girl waiting for him.

Garland laughed, threw her gloves up onto his chest, and then she snatched his hand. He hadn't even realized his fingers were cold until she took them in her knitted grip.

"Not bad," she said in an encouraging tone. "I'm impressed." She looped her arm through his and pulled him along, showing him how to correct his footing and pointing out other skaters who knew what they were doing. He wobbled several times over scrapes in the ice but managed to stay upright even though he gasped out loud and had to spin his arms like a clock to keep from falling.

They skated for what seemed like hours, laughing and talking about some of their favorite things about Christmas. Pete wondered if Garland realized she was admitting them. She told him how her mother baked cookies every year and took the family caroling whether they wanted to go or not.

"You have no idea how much I miss that now," she laughed, "even though I know I can't sing a note."

He told her about a holiday he spent in Colorado, and how the city there had an enormous sleigh with real reindeer, all wearing red harnesses and bells. "The look on the children's faces," he said with a shake of his head, "was like they were witnessing magic for the first time."

Garland pointed toward the gazebo just when Pete thought his hips might stiffen for good. "Do you want to go inside and sit? I really want to see that tree."

He agreed, and they made their way over, careful not to crash into any other skaters. Once he reached the steps, Pete heaved a sigh of relief and reached for the railing. "I can't believe I haven't fallen once."

"Neither can I, but the night is young." Garland raised a brow. "I used to skate several times a year, but this is Thorpes, we can do that here."

Pete felt rather proud of himself. "We don't have this in Florida, well, unless you're into hockey." They clomped up the stairs and chose one of the curved benches around the Christmas tree to sit down on and relax.

Garland dropped his hand and plopped down beside him. They watched the other skaters circle the rink for a while then Pete turned toward the decorated blue spruce in the center of the porch.

"Wow," he said, examining a life-sized blue jay. "That looks so real."

"It's just feathers, but yes, they look real. See there, that's a cuckoo, and that sweet one there is a dove."

"I know that's a hummingbird." Pete pointed at the tree.

"Yes," she agreed, "although you won't see those in the winter. They don't stay around in these temperatures." She continued to examine the tree closely, lost in thought.

Pete sat back and looked at the natural-looking nests entwined in the branches. A wide blue and silver ribbon circled the tree from top to bottom. "We have flamingos. They've always amused me, but they're arrogant buggers, and parrots? Cripes, you can't shut them up."

Garland laughed. "You've never been surrounded by a horde of crows then."

"Not that I recall, but don't get me wrong—I do love them—birds. They're amazing to watch in flight. In fact," he admitted in a quiet voice, "I always wanted to be one."

He sensed her watching him and turned to look. Their faces were so close Pete could see small flecks of violet in her eyes. Her nose was straight, and a deep dip at the top of her upper lip looked like someone had put their finger there and pressed down. And then there was her mouth. Her lips were smooth and shined like she'd just licked them, or maybe it was a cherry colored-lip gloss. It accentuated the bloom in her cheeks.

"What?" Pete realized he was staring and thinking more than friendly thoughts. "I'm sorry." He cleared his throat but didn't sit back. He liked the closeness.

"Hey," said Garland, cracking the mood before it hung too heavy between them, "Let's do one more lap around the rink and then go find something to eat."

"That sounds like a plan."

She jumped up, and he followed her back down the gazebo steps making good use of the railing. When they hit bottom, the ice felt glassy under his feet, and he found himself hanging on her arm for balance.

"What's the matter, Darling?" laughed Garland. She shook free from his hand and began to skate in circles around him, gliding across the ice as easily as a breeze rippled over a pond.

"I think the cold is not my friend," Pete chuckled. He realized he felt tired and his concentration fading.

"And I was so impressed," pouted Garland. She glided by him just inches away, and he wobbled. She chuckled then flew around him in another circle.

The fence around the rink made a nice barrier, but more importantly, it was something to hold onto. Pete lined himself up in its direction and slid his way across the ice, relishing the freedom of floating over the ground's surface but wary of his weakening balance.

Two giggling girls crossed in front of him, and he nearly landed on top of them. They screeched and hurried ahead which left him barreling forward into the wall. His arms flayed out to keep his balance.

Garland almost cried laughing so hard. He crashed into the fence, and his feet slipped out from under him, but he managed to hold on and only dangle ungracefully before getting them back beneath himself.

Giggling, Garland reached out to the fence to hold on so she could double over and laugh harder.

"Ha-ha! Pete Darling, Mr. Action Adventure and businessman extraordinaire," she cried. "You're just like everyone else on the ice."

He chuckled, his breath blowing out in a giant cloud. "For my first time, you have to admit that was pretty amazing. And I still have my dignity."

She smiled at him as the laughter died down. Her eyes gleamed from the sparkling lights overhead.

"Actually, you did pretty well. Let me guess, you rollerblade or skateboard."

"Both," he boasted, unable to help himself, "and I've never broken anything." He turned his attention to dusting off his shoulders and arms.

"Well, a couple more seasons in Thorpes, and you'll be a pro."

Wondering what she meant or if she meant anything at all, Pete straightened, put his back to the fence, and scooted closer beside her.

"That sounds like fun," he said casually. She fell quiet like she was embarrassed at her own words. He looked over and caught her gaze. She straightened her lips together in a serious line, but he could still see a faint smile clinging to the corners of her mouth.

"You really like it here, don't you?" she asked.

Her face radiated a wintry glow and something that looked like contentment. A lone, drifting snowflake billowed across her cheek, and Pete looked up to see the sky dripping with lace polka dots.

"I do." Unable to resist, he let a little of his heart show. "I like a lot of things about Thorpes and a lot of people here, too."

She held his gaze, and he felt encouraged to continue. "Like, Lynette at the Blackberry Inn, and Rhea, who I always run into at the bookstore, and I see Monty at the bakery, and Darren down at the airport. He's a pro with the vending machines. Then there's..." he hesitated and balled his fist under his chin and pretended to think.

Garland's mouth twitched to hold back a smile.

"Let's see. There's also a girl at the Lava Java." He looked sideways at her. "You know what?"

"What?" Her voice sounded light, almost inaudible, and she looked breathless. The snowflakes floated down faster now.

"She's one of the strongest and most beautiful people I've ever met." He furrowed his brows. "She's smart, too, but stubborn. "

Garland grimaced and grinned at the same time.

"Oh, she's stubborn, alright," he repeated with a shake of his head.

"Maybe she just has plans."

Pete turned to face Garland. With one move, he could sweep her into his arms, except he was on slippery skates. "Maybe," he said in a soft voice, "she thinks she needs plans so she won't end up trapped in a town with friends and family she doesn't realize she needs and loves."

The smiled dropped from Garland's face. A painful pause followed. "Pete, it's not that I don't love my family, but..." She looked up. "I can't count on them, and I..." Her eyes watered, and she blinked and looked away.

"You were left to care for your mother alone, and no one was there for you and it was devasting. You don't want to get hurt again. I get it."

When her gaze returned, he looked deep into her eyes. "Only the people we love can really hurt us," he acknowledged, "but sometimes it's best to try and understand and give them another chance. You only get one family, Garland."

She bit her lip but gave him an understanding look. "I know, and I know you don't really have one or something like that."

"I don't have any family, not anymore, and I know what it's like to have regrets when everyone's gone."

Garland exhaled. "It's just you and your inheritance, huh?"

He nodded. "And it hasn't made me very happy." Pete stopped, then confessed, "Well, not until it brought me here."

She seemed to understand the compliment and didn't look like she wanted to push him away or run off. In fact, Garland looked like she might feel something for him, too. The tough exterior melted away, and she looked unguarded.

"I—," she said, her gaze flitting between his eyes and mouth. "I think a part of you belongs here."

Pete watched her lips move, hesitated, and knew if he didn't kiss her he'd regret it the rest of his life. With a small breath of courage, he leaned in and brushed his mouth over hers, his mind shooting up to the night sky and the rest of him swirling and glowing. He was flying. She tasted like peppermint and promise, both exciting and comforting at the same time. Without thinking, his grip left the fence, and he wrapped his arms around her. His heart took over his body.

"Peter!" A sharp, shrill voice cracked the air and yanked him out of the most romantic moment of his life. "Pete Darling!" cried the angry, maternal tone.

With his mouth hanging open in surprise, feeling stupid and not very debonair, Pete turned toward Bella's familiar voice. She stood on the ice not five feet away wearing white, downy mittens. She looked like a toothpick coated in faux fur trim. Even her skates glowed white like she'd brought them herself.

He almost laughed, except he'd heard Garland's sharp intake of breath.

"What do you think you're doing?"

"I'm skating. I told you I was going skating tonight." He glanced at Garland and saw her staring at Bella like she'd seen a ghost.

"This is—"

"Garland, I know." Bella sounded angry, not just annoyed.

"I didn't know you'd met," he said, wondering if his secretary had been checking things out behind his back. "I thought you were on your way back to New York."

"When you said you were going skating," she said icily, "I assumed you were going this afternoon and that you would be alone."

"I see," he said, an ache pinching his back between his shoulders. Bella was becoming a nuisance. She never could differentiate between his personal and business life.

"I don't need a babysitter," he said, his ire rising. "I appreciate you coming out and taking care of the schedule and invoices in person, but I only have a couple weeks left and the job will be done."

Bella's glare shifted to Garland. "You could have been finished much earlier if you'd devoted all of your time to the job."

He gave her a warning stare. "You knew I had other things to do." From the corner of his eye, he saw Garland's face jerk toward him then back at Bella like she was watching a ping-pong match.

Bella parted her red painted lips and tapped her white teeth together.

"I should go," said Garland. "I have a—"

"Yes," agreed Bella, "you should go."

Garland froze, her hand on the fence. The snow was falling faster and thicker now.

"Wait," said Pete. He covered her gloves with his palm. "Please." He shot Bella a stormy glare. "Lest you get the wrong idea," he explained to Garland in a loud tone, "this is my secretary, Bella Barrie, who's in town taking care of business for me, but she's leaving."

"We've met," responded Garland.

He raised a brow and turned back to his annoying employee. She had the nerve to stand there looking like an angry wife. He'd seen it before, lots of times, but this time it wasn't cute or funny or impish at all.

"I'll speak with you when I get back to Florida," he said in a dismissive tone. Bella's arms were still crossed. She glared, her face beet red and glowing like Rudolph's nose under the Christmas lights. "It's time for you to leave," Pete enunciated.

Garland pulled away and skated off. He took an exasperated breath, threw Bella an angry glare, and hurried after her. Unfortunately, that meant he no longer had the fence behind his back and there was no one to hold onto. His skate hit a hole in the ice, and the momentum took him up into the air while his arms wind-milled around like a cartoon character. He fell and landed with a bone-crunching pain on his backside as his eyes slammed shut with pain.

It was the last glimpse he had of the girl he was falling for. Ironically.

CHAPTER SIX

Garland could not bear the thought of going to work the next morning. She decided to hibernate in her apartment until it was time to take her final exams that night. Her legs felt exhausted and sore from skating. Her heart felt bruised.

Whatever had happened between Pete and the glowering woman in white had been awkward and uncomfortable. Garland grimaced, cursed the holiday music echoing in her mind, and wondered if he'd gone out for pizza without her.

She should have stayed, she knew. It wasn't like he'd be here forever. No matter how much he enjoyed the ambiance of Thorpes, he'd head back to Florida in his fancy car to his mysterious and exciting life soon.

Too bad she admired him and was ridiculously attracted to him. And that kiss.

She fell backward on the bed and stared at the whitewashed beadboard on the ceiling. Her heart skipped a beat and then another for good measure. Maybe it was the lights or the music or just the contagious holiday spirit in the air, but his lips on hers had tuned out everything around them and made her heart catch fire and melt her bones. It was magical and sweet, and at the same time, sizzling and stomach-clenching. She'd felt like she floated away into a dream.

Until Bella.

Garland felt her face twist into a scowl. She reminded her of a sultry angel hiding a black heart. What kind of woman, or secretary for that matter, showed up on her boss's date and threw a temper tantrum?

She felt certain Bella was more than an employee. That was for sure, and it explained everything. Garland stretched for her phone. Earlier, she'd called the Inn, convinced Lynette to give her Pete's number, then texted him and apologized for leaving. Of course, she'd fibbed and said she was going straight to bed so there wouldn't be any awkward phone calls.

She checked her messages. He'd sent two. *I'm so sorry*, he'd said in one. The next asked, *Coffee tomorrow?*

He didn't even like coffee. Garland closed her eyes and took a deep breath. Her mind swirled with confusion. Maybe it'd be better to call into work and take some time away from the situation. She was acting like a girl in love, and that couldn't be, because she had another semester of school working an internship along the eastern seaboard as soon as she could find one. Next stop? Her own business and the chance to be a rip-roaring success—far away from Thorpes where she could put the pain of her mother's death behind her and start fresh.

Her phone made a chiming sound, and her heart leapt into her throat. She looked down at the screen and saw Mariah's name.

Let's go shopping.

Shopping? Garland didn't have a ton of money. She pinched every dime for school. But it was Christmas. She sighed. Dad had texted again, and Joy had emailed to ask her if she wanted to come to dinner Christmas Eve. Garland hadn't replied. She hadn't thought of a good enough excuse, but she would. They all knew she would.

She thought of her father and the last time she'd seen him. It was last summer. They lived twenty-five minutes apart, but she hadn't dropped by the house or gone to the family's church in years. She even avoided the stores they all frequented and slipped out the backdoor of the café if she saw one of them wander in.

Okay. She answered Mariah with one simple word. Although it would mean Doug would be running the café for half the day, she knew her mother would be appalled if she didn't get her father a Christmas present.

Last year, she'd sent him a fruit basket. She chewed her lip, ashamed. She'd sent him something from a catalog like he lived a thousand miles away. But really, she excused herself, she was only as far away from him as he'd put himself away from his wife when she'd fallen ill.

Wiping her hands over her face, Garland knew she could do better. She was acting like a child. Pete would tell her that, too, if he knew. He'd be flabbergasted that she hadn't bought any Christmas gifts yet.

Crawling out of the bed, she headed for the shower to get ready for the hour-long drive to the closest shopping mall. Maybe, she thought, she'd wear the little candy cane earrings.

MARIAH PICKED HER UP before noon, and they drove down the highway singing Christmas rock songs and squinting in bright sunlight. The first real snowfall of the year had dropped a respectable three inches, but more was on the way.

"We're lucky the snowplows were out last night."

"Mm-hmm," said Mariah, "and the sun is out. It's melted off the roads now, but we still have plenty in the yard so Ella is having a good time."

"Darren didn't mind you taking off work to spend time with me?"

Mariah laughed. "Not if I'm buying him something for Christmas. I'd like to check and see if I can find anything with unicorns for Ella. She's easy."

Garland grinned. "Cute. I wish I would have had little sisters. All I ever bought was metal cars for my brothers every year. So boring."

Mariah winked. "You may have a girl to buy for someday."

"You're getting ahead of yourself," Garland groaned, "way ahead."

"You never know. How did the date go last night?"

Garland focused on the blur of trees whizzing past her car window. "It went fine. We skated, we talked, and then his secretary showed up and that was that."

"His secretary?"

Garland glanced across the seat. "Remember Miss Bella Barrie?"

"You're kidding. The tall woman with an endless supply of sunglasses that sneaks in every Saturday morning and orders like an auctioneer?"

"Yes, the very one, and I'm glad I'm not around for that. I guess she came to town to help him with paperwork or something, but last night she showed up right when... Well, worse timing ever."

Mariah raised a brow. "What exactly is bad timing?"

Garland's cheeks warmed and a small chuckle squeaked out and became a giggle.

"You didn't."

"No!" she exclaimed with a flush. "Maybe. It just happened, and it was wonderful until that screeching barn owl showed up and shamed him like he was a ten-year-old boy. Talk about weird."

"She sounds a little overprotective if you ask me."

"Mm," grunted Garland.

Mariah guided her small van off a freeway exit, and they pulled into the mall less than a mile away. The parking lot was filled all the way to the main road so they had to walk some distance in the cold, but Garland didn't mind.

Sunshine made icicles shimmer like glitter and took the chill out of the air. Heated sidewalks made it easy to walk from outside into the lobby, and once inside the mall, Garland caught herself humming along with a rustic version of a holiday homecoming song. She had to leave off the last few words of the chorus. She'd never come home for Christmas and see her mother again.

Sensing her mood, Mariah took her by the elbow, and they walked side by side into a thick throng of holiday shoppers dressed in festive colors. Laughter and excited chatter rose above the piped music. The splashing sound of a fountain waterfall chimed in, and Garland followed her nose to popcorn popping in a giant, old-fashioned kettle outside the entrance to an indoor movie theater.

"This is nice," she said.

Mariah pointed at one of the children's stores. "I don't mind shopping if I have a purpose, but I really don't care for crowds and concrete."

"But look," argued Garland, "there's a gingerbread house and all kinds of Christmas trees. You should have brought Ella to see Santa."

Mariah jerked her head back and stared. "Who are you? We're taking her on Christmas Eve. Why are you suddenly in the Christmas spirit?"

Garland smiled. "Oh, I don't know." She shrugged. "It's just... nice. Everyone's thinking about others, and there's fun stuff to see and do. I actually came along to see if I could find something for my father."

"That's nice. I'm glad to hear it."

"Joy, too," added Garland. "She keeps texting me asking me if I'm going to the Yuletide Ball which means she'll be in town. She'll probably come by my apartment."

"Are you?" Mariah pulled her into an upscale children's shop and started browsing through red and silver toddler dresses.

"Me?" Garland pointed at a green dress with white stripes. "That would look cute on her."

"Yes, it would, but don't change the subject. Are you going to the ball with a certain Lava Java customer?"

Garland snorted. "No. I don't think he even knows about it, and I'm sure he'll be done and gone by then."

"What do you mean? It's just a week and a half away."

"If Bella Barrie has anything to do with it, they'll be back in Florida by then."

"Ugh," said Mariah for her.

They picked out a dress that was on sale, and Mariah let Garland buy Ella a pair of matching stockings, then they set out down the promenade of shops looking for more ideas. At a candle shop, Garland bought a nice candle for Joy that smelled like butter cookies, and in another, she found a bottle of cologne for her father. A plate of brownies from the coffee shop would have to do for her brothers—if she saw them at all.

She pushed the uneasiness she felt away. In the back of her mind, she'd almost decided to stop by and see the family at Christmas. She'd avoided them all since the funeral, and each passing year just made it worse.

"Wow," said Mariah, cutting through the swirl of anxiety in her mind. Garland looked in the direction she pointed. A large department store at the end of the mall had mannequins dressed in party dresses, and sale signs were everywhere.

"Do you want a dress?"

"No," said Mariah, pushing her forward, "you do."

Garland shook her head. "I don't need a party dress. I have a little black one that does just fine if I need a reason to wear one."

"Exactly. You have one nice dress, and you hardly ever wear it. What if you do go to the Christmas dance? It's a ball. You'll need something spectacular."

"Why?" groaned Garland. "I don't have a date, and I'm not that spectacular."

"Are you kidding?" Mariah swatted her on the arm. "You're practically an assistant manager, you go to school full-time, you volunteer for the community, and you're graduating in less than a year. You're amazing."

"I still need an internship," Garland reminded her, "and I'm a little old for a graduate."

"You're never too old," argued her friend.

Reluctantly, Garland allowed herself to be dragged into an aisle of scarlet floor-length ball gowns. "Well, at least I'll be finished with school soon and out of Thorpes."

"Don't remind me," said Mariah with a sigh. "I honestly don't know what I'll do without you. I can hardly function now." She picked up a gleaming blue silk dress with a snug bodice and tulle skirt and held it up like a trophy.

"You've got to be kidding," Garland groaned. Glitter sparkled across its shoulders.

"This is amazing. It'll make your eyes look cobalt blue."

"It looks like a dress for Cinderella."

Mariah shoved the hanger into her stomach. "Every girl should dress up like Cinderella at least once in her lifetime. Go put it on. Now."

Garland obeyed with a grunt. She'd prefer something a little shorter and less flouncy, but it was a breathtaking gown. She dug deep for another dose of Christmas spirit and sighed. "Why not," she muttered to herself. She peeled off her jeans and heavy sweater in the dressing room then tugged the gown over her head. When it slid over her face and settled on her shoulders, she stared in surprise.

The blue made her fair complexion glow, and Mariah was right—it did make her blue eyes look darker. She pulled her hair off of her neck and gazed in the mirror. If she made an effort, she could look amazing. She wondered how Pete would react if he saw her at her finest.

A price tag spun in slow circles from where it was attached under the dress's arm sleeve. Garland grabbed for it, amused at herself for considering such a silly expense for something she would never wear more than once or twice.

"How does it look?" Mariah's voice echoed through the dressing room.

Garland stared at the tag. "It looks expensive that's what it looks like."

"Don't be ridiculous, I'm buying it."

"No." Garland dropped the tag and let her shoulders slump. She stood on her toes and tried to peer over the top of the dressing room door at her friend, but she was too short. "It's way over budget."

"It's my gift to you."

Garland yanked open the door and stalked out. "You don't have the extra money to buy me a dress! Besides, I've never spent more than seventy-five dollars on something to wear."

"You're cheap." Mariah stopped teasing and stared. The room fell oddly silent.

"You're making me self-conscious."

"You look amazing."

Garland turned back to the mirror and examined herself again. Mariah came up behind her in the reflection. "Let's go in halves," her boss insisted. "You need this dress."

Staring at herself made Garland realize she hadn't really dressed up in a long time—not since before Mom had died.

Pete made her feel like she was waking up from a long, heavy sleep and was ready to embrace life. Their simple ice skating date had been a really fun time. He'd listened, sympathized, encouraged, and even teased her. Then he'd kissed her like—well, like no one had ever kissed her before, that was for sure. He was a total stranger who blew into town with his sappy smiles, probing questions, and endless positive cheer. Something about him made her want to believe in fairytales.

"I'll take the dress."

PETE DID ONE FINAL walk around the Cessna to make sure he'd wiped off all of the stray smudges. The airplane looked spotless on the outside and was in perfect working order on the inside. With a sigh of satisfaction, he walked across the hanger to pick up the last of the paperwork and file it away. Next week, besides a new dial to install, he just had a few remaining checks on the prop plane next door.

He slapped the blue file down and looked around the hanger. It was heated although little drafts seeped in from the hanger doors, but with his jumpsuit over his clothes, he stayed warm enough. The little workshop was beginning to feel like home.

Pete rubbed his hands together and glanced through the small window over the hanger door. Outside, the sun had set and runway lights twinkled on the snowy ground making it look like a distant city. His stomach made a complaining noise, and he realized he looked forward to dinner at the inn. Lynette had promised everyone pot roast and vegetables with homemade bread that morning, and it had driven him along all afternoon.

He'd kept busy trying to push the upcoming weekend from his mind and not hang around the coffee shop too much. Garland had been out the couple of times he dropped by. She'd thanked him for the night out and said nothing about Bella. He knew she was busy finishing school and probably needed time off for her tests. All of it should be over by the weekend. Maybe they could talk again—or something more.

The tapping of shoes in the distance made Pete lean over to look. It was getting late, and the office was probably ready to lock up. He unzipped the mechanic's jumpsuit protecting his clothes and stumbled around as he worked his way out of it, but not before the door adjacent to the office building opened, and Bella strode through.

This evening she sported black trousers and a short jacket with a red silk blouse. Her shoes were half-boots and half sharp heels—stylish but dangerous looking. Her bright lipstick matched her shirt.

"You didn't send me the final report," she said, tapping her phone back and forth in her hand. Platinum and diamond earrings swung in her earlobes. "I'm flying out for good tomorrow," she added with pursed lips, "but don't worry. I have business in Lawrenceburg, so I'm staying at my hotel one more night before driving back up to New York."

Pete turned back for the file folder on the table. "I've just finished up here if you want to scan and file this one." They hadn't spoken since the night at the ice skating rink where she'd suddenly appeared like a shepherding dog.

Bella approached him, her chin high and face grim. "How much longer on the remaining plane? I need to know whether you'll be here or home in Miami by Christmas."

"Just fax everything to the apartment," answered Pete. "I'll be home soon."

"Not soon enough," she murmured like silk. She took the file folder.

Pete stopped to examine her styled hair and soft cheeks. "I know you don't like the cold," he said, trying to sound gracious. "It doesn't bother me. To be honest, I don't even know why I stay in Florida other than it reminds me of the islands. It'd make more sense to move to the central part of the country since I'm all over the place."

"Or L.A.," she said, without missing a beat.

"It's really not for me. You know that. I'd feel like I'm on the edge of the world, and it's twice as far to London."

Bella pressed the file up against her chest, her long nails tapping the edges of it like she was playing an instrument. "You haven't flown home in over five years. I didn't think it mattered to you anymore."

"It matters," Pete said defensively. "It's just there's nothing there. The money is wired. The family—the rest of the Darlings—are here, minus only a few cousins in Michigan and Mr. Hagel in Boca Raton."

Bella snorted. "He's a hundred and two. He'll outlive us all, and he's hardly related."

Pete shrugged. "Son of a butler or something. It's fine. He has the nicest room in the senior center near the ocean."

She sighed. "You are a prince. If you weren't so worried about spreading around the Darling's wealth, you could live like a king, and I mean that quite literally."

He smiled. "I already do, and what do I need it all for? It sits in those hidden accounts and grows and grows while I have my own career like I always wanted."

"Well, you could give your longest and oldest employee a raise." She sniffed.

He chuckled. "You make more than any secretary I know, Bella, and thank you. I do appreciate all you do for me."

She pressed her lips together and gave a loud sigh. "I know what you're thinking and that you're upset with me." She gave him a matronly nod that reminded him of a schoolteacher. "I'm just watching out for you like I always have. Remember Leslie Keaton? If it weren't for me, that little wretch would have tied you around her finger and bilked you for every penny you're worth."

Pete threw back his head and laughed. "Oh, Bella, she was great fun. I was just enjoying her company. I knew she wasn't in love with me or anything like that. She was a great girl and a good friend."

"With very expensive hobbies she liked you to pay for."

He shrugged. "I didn't mind. It amused me."

"Well, I wasn't amused," said Bella darkly. "You have to be careful. Some people can smell money from a mile away, and they're happy to live off you if they can get away with it."

"Aw," he waved her off. "You worry too much."

Bella stared at him, and her pale eyes seemed to darken a little. "It's my job to protect you and your money."

He gave his head a small shake. "My money's not in danger here. This is a nice town with nice people."

Her cheeks pinkened, and she frowned. "You're practically related to them, almost, which is why you shouldn't get attached."

"You mean Garland."

Bella tapped the file Pete had handed her against her leg. "Of course I do. You've been doling out anonymous gifts and watching her family for years. She's a proud girl and wouldn't want to know that you paid for her mother's care and even her Aunt Grace's now."

Pete dropped his eyes to the floor. Would Garland find it odd? Would she be angry to learn he'd inherited all of her great-great grandmother's family money and turned it into billions? He was trying to make it right. Being a young boy with money and responsibilities made one grow up fast.

"Look," he said giving Bella a small smile, "you don't need to worry. I just have a few more repairs on the other plane, and I'll be back in Miami before you know it."

"Good." Bella narrowed her eyes. "Because you don't belong up here in the middle of nowhere with these people. This town is like a walk-in greeting card. Did you know there were children, literally dozens of them, staring in the storefront windows smudging the glass with runny noses yesterday looking at toys? I could hardly get by to get into the salon—if that's what you want to call it."

She shuddered, and Pete laughed.

"Bella," he chided her, "you really should spend less time on Rodeo Drive."

"No," she disagreed, "that's exactly where I should spend time. Tomorrow I'll drive back to New York, turn in my car, and fly home." She looked at him pointedly. "Promise me that's exactly what you'll do before Christmas. I'll find you a children's wing in a hospital somewhere so you don't get blue."

He smiled at her even though a dull ache began to throb in the back of his head. "Sounds wonderful," he replied. She gave him a prim wave, and he watched her saunter out. Her figure and her antics were familiar to him, but now any attractive woman he looked at just brought Garland to mind.

Something intense and admirable and yes, beautiful, about her had caught his attention the first moment he'd seen her. It'd been hard to keep his distance, and he'd secretly looked forward to bumping into her in the coffee shop to make sure she and her family were well, but things had escalated and so quickly.

Once she was over her suspicions of him, she made him admire her all the more for her protectiveness of her aunt, her sacrifice putting off her education to care for her mother, and her commitment to her education and dreams, no matter how late she felt they were for her. Not to mention, the way she treated others around her and her loyalty to Mariah.

He just wanted to know her more, and of course, although the kiss had been irrational and impulsive, it'd been the best first kiss of his life and magical, too, because it meant something. The thought that it would also be the last made his head hurt even more.

CHAPTER SEVEN

Garland felt like she'd finished a marathon after her last final. She slept late the next morning then showered and dressed for work. The coffee shop would be as busy as ever with Christmas only a week away. She hadn't seen Pete all week and wondered if he'd left town. The ache to see him gave her stomach drunken butterflies, but they practically fell to her toes when she walked in the front door.

There he sat at his corner bistro table in a dark gray coat she hadn't seen before. A black knit scarf to fight off the dropping temperatures was draped over the chair next to him. His turquoise eyes found hers, and she realized he'd seen her come in.

Maybe he'd been waiting for her. He'd sent her a message wishing her luck with her tests. She'd sent him a smiley face and then before she could change her mind, a heart. She forced herself to only give him a brisk wave and hurry to the kitchen. Mariah put her hands on her chest with relief when she saw her, and they worked the muffins and anxious demands for hot apple cider for the next hour and a half.

Friends and neighbors came and went, their arms filled with colorful shopping bags and stomping snow off of their boots at the door. Christmas lights blinked in the windows making the café a bit more magical. The Christmas music was low, sometimes pop and sometimes reverent hymns, and more than once Garland caught herself peeking to see if Pete had left.

Mariah nodded Pete's direction. "He's been here a long time," she whispered.

Garland concentrated on blending up Rhea's frappe. "He's reading a book. And he ordered a muffin a half hour ago."

"Okay," teased Mariah. "He's just really into his book." She arched a brow, and Garland ignored her.

As the customers thinned out, she wiped down the front counter and then headed for the nearest table. When she'd cleaned her way to the window, Pete had his book face-down on the table and his chin in his hand. "How'd the final exams go?"

Garland smiled, picked up an abandoned saucer, and walked over to him. "I'm done at last."

"So you're really going to leave Thorpes and move to the city?"

Her smile faded. "What can I do? I need an internship, and there's not anything around."

Pete bit his lip. "You could start your business here."

"I will someplace else," she said, "after I get my diploma."

"I admire your dedication."

"Thanks. It's been a long road."

"Your family must be really proud of you."

Again, he cut her where it counted. "Thanks. I bought my father something for Christmas."

"You did? That's nice."

"Thanks." He smiled at her, and she wondered why she wanted to blab all of her personal details. "It's just, I haven't done much for anyone since my mother died." A lump swelled up out of nowhere in Garland's throat. "She just loved Christmas. It was crazy. She'd start decorating in September after school started—inside the house at least." She broke into giggles as her eyes welled up. "It used to drive us nuts."

Pete smiled so wide it reached his ears. He pushed the chair beside him over to her. "Please," he said. "Tell me. I've never decorated for Christmas before."

"What about your family?"

He shrugged. "Foster care, remember? Then a guardian. Not a big deal."

"I'm sorry." Garland swiped at her eyes. "You know, I've always been so annoyed with her for giving me such a ridiculous name."

"Well it could have been worse, like Icicle or something."

She laughed again. "You're right. We have a Joy, Nick, and a Christopher. I guess I won the creative one."

He winked at her. It made her feel warm all over. "Do you know it's really a compliment?"

She gasped. "Being named after a decoration?"

Pete reached out and took her hand to play with her fingers. "No, I mean being named after a garland—a wreath. Cultures and religious all over the world use them as symbols of peace and purity."

"I've never really thought about that before."

He nodded. "Your mother must have really loved you."

That did it. A tear welled up and escaped out of the corner of her eye. Garland glanced down at her fingers entwined in his and swallowed the painful lump in her throat down. "She did," she admitted in a pained voice. "We were close. We both loved reading and baking. She bragged to everyone about my good grades in school. We both loved birds." She chuckled. "I donated one of her little crafts to the town Christmas tree. That's why I was studying it so closely the night we went skating.

"Oh, I see." Pete reached up and dried the dampness on her cheek.

"When she got sick, I'd just started school, but I had to drop out. Joy was married, the boys threw themselves into their friends and sports, and my father just..." She sat up as something became clear in her mind. "He didn't know what to do," she said slowly. "He stayed late at work or he'd sit in the room with her and just stare. Eventually, I did everything and when the hospital sent her home I..."

A sob wanted to escape, but Garland made herself say it. "I guess I did it all and resented it. Not her," she said quickly, "but my family. No one knew how to help, and I didn't know how not to. It drained me, and afterward, I just didn't want to see them or be reminded of what I'd gone through."

She searched his eyes to see if he understood, and he seemed to. Pete squeezed her hand. "You are a wonderful, loyal, and hardworking person," he whispered. He sat up and took a deep breath. "Can I say something?"

"Sure."

"Do you know what I think is the best thing you could give your father for Christmas?"

"What's that?"

"Forgiveness."

Garland sniffled. "You're right. That would be the right thing to do. For all of them."

Pete nodded. "I know it's easy for me to say because I'm not in the situation. Just call me an observer who can see the trees within the forest."

Garland glanced down at his hand over hers. It felt warm and comfortable and safe. "What about you, Pete? Have you ever had to forgive someone like that?"

"Sure. It was a long time before I didn't resent my birth parents for leaving me an orphan. And, well... we all have family stories." He glanced at her then looked away.

"I'd like to hear those sometime." Garland peered over her shoulder and saw that no one was minding the front counter. She realized there was so much more about Pete she wanted to learn. The glittering blue ball gown hanging in her closet seemed to call out. She suddenly wanted desperately for him to see her in it.

"Pete," she said, her chest nearly seizing with anxiety, "did you know there's a ball this weekend? The Yuletide Ball?"

"I heard about it." He hesitated like he was thinking then pointed at the curled flyer still hanging onto the coffee shop's front window. "I hate to miss it."

"When do you go home?"

"I should be finished up by Thursday night," Pete stammered. He looked away like he didn't want to talk about it; like he didn't want to go or for her to invite him. Garland tried not to feel crestfallen. She could take a hint.

Pete looked out the window at the Christmas lights blinking up and down the street. "I'm sure it will be magical."

"It usually is," said Garland. "I guess I've taken it for granted all these years." She forced a smile and tried not to think about the fact that last week's first kiss would be their only one. He'd swept into town like a prince, but it was all too good to be true. Her Christmas fairy tale romance was over.

A heavy blanket of sadness settled over her shoulders, but she pulled them back and straightened up. "Tell me," she said sliding her hand out from under his and pulling away. "What do they do at Christmas in Miami?"

PETE DAWDLED IN HIS room up until the last moments before checkout then carried his bag downstairs. He should have been homesick and ready to return to the warmer climate, but he wasn't. His stomach churned, and his heart felt like a brick.

Garland had all but asked him to stay, but he couldn't. Bella had warned him, and he'd promised her he wouldn't get involved.

Lynette was on the phone but raised a hand for him to stop as he trudged down the last carpeted stair into the lobby. She hung up shortly after he stood near the door, examining the blankets of deep snow that had fallen during the night covering the street.

"Are you sure you're going to be safe?" The bed and breakfast owner strode out in her slacks and heavy sweater wearing a pair of water and snow boots. She pointed out the window. "It snowed three more inches last night, and it's pretty cold. I don't think this is going to melt off for you."

He nodded. "Don't worry. My car can handle it."

She made a noise of concern but picked up one of his bags and insisted on helping him to the car with it. Pete reached out a hand to shake, and she laughed, gave him a hug, and told him to come back. He promised he would, but it made him feel sick because he had no idea when that would be. Where would Garland be by then?

The day looked black, white, and still. The highway was coated in smooth powder, the trees wet and dark, and the sky gray. Soon, the nice retirement home appeared out of the gloom on his right, and Pete slowed and turned in.

He'd shut off the self-driving mechanism on the electric car. His feelings about the novelty had changed. It was ridiculous to ride along with no effort to where he was going. If he was going to be in charge of his life, he needed to act like it instead of going with the flow and floating along on the wind stream of his money and toys. He'd thought he'd given up everything when he decided it was time to grow up, but he knew now that meant more than being a man with a good career and paying back his dues by watching over the Darling family inheritance. Truly living meant being willing to give up his heart.

He plowed through the snow in the parking lot and hurried into the lobby looking slyly about for security. Seeing no one, he waited until the front desk help was busy with the family in front of him juggling large presents for their grandpa, and when no one was looking, scurried down the hall to Aunt Grace's room.

She was sitting at the window in her wheelchair with her eyes closed. Wondering if the open curtains were letting in a chill, he crept in beside her and reached up to shut them.

"Leave them open," she said, breaking the quiet. He jumped. Slowly, she opened her eyes. Pete backed up and sat in a chair against the wall across from her.

"I thought you were napping."

Garland's great aunt loosened a small smile. "I was waiting for you."

"You were?"

She chuckled soft and low. "You always come at Christmas, Peter. In one way or another."

"You know it's Christmas?"

"Of course, I do. There's snow and lights and people bring me presents." She hesitated. "It's hot and sunny on my birthday."

Pete leaned forward and took Grace's hand. "I'm glad you remember your birthday. And me."

She squeezed his fingers with her warm, gentle hands. "How could I forget you, Peter? You were always there when I needed you most. You always have been."

He tried to bite back a modest smile, but it came anyway.

"Thank you for taking care of me and my niece. Garland, too."

"Yes. Garland's mother had a hard time of it, but she endured to the end. Crossed over to the next star." He smiled at her and glanced out the window. Another star. Another life. Just a memory now.

"I like Garland, Aunt Grace," he admitted. He found himself biting the side of his lip as he looked toward the door in case an orderly came by.

"Yes, Garland, my little one," said the wise and crinkled woman.

"She watches out for you."

Grace nodded. "Yes, like you. And I watch out for her." She turned her head to face him and gave him a quizzical stare. "Who will take care of Garland when I'm gone? She thinks she doesn't need anybody."

"I will," he promised.

"Will you?"

He nodded, meaning every word of it. "I promise."

This seemed to placate Grace, and she inhaled deeply and let it out, her gaze returning to the wintry scene outside. "Where does the sun go when the snow comes?"

The answer was so obvious he wasn't sure if he should give it, but then Grace dropped her head back against the headrest. "The same place as the stars," she murmured. With a jerk, she turned her gaze back to him. "When are you going home, Peter? Are you coming with me?"

He studied her a few seconds and seeing her sincerity replied, "I have to stay here now, Aunt Grace. I can't go back anymore, at least, until it's time for me to fly away."

"Then you'll stay here? In Thorpes? And watch over the family for me?"

"Of course I will," he said automatically. His chest squeezed. Then why was he going back to Florida? There was nothing there.

"You can stay at my house," said Grace, sinking back into her chair and closing her eyes again. "You stay there, Peter Darling. This is your new home."

Or maybe it was "Peter, darling," he thought, when he kissed her on the cheek, left the gift bag of mints on her table, and snuck out without being seen.

Grace wouldn't be around much longer. He knew it, could feel it, and more importantly, he trusted that Wendy Darling's granddaughter knew far more than he did about what should be done. He trudged back to the car and sat inside waiting for it to warm up, staring at the highway on the other side of the parking lot. One end pointed toward Florida. The other pointed back up the road to Thorpes.

GARLAND PARKED OUTSIDE the community center, feeling ridiculous driving an old beat-up hatchback and wearing a long coat over her gown. Mariah had talked her into going to the salon and paying good money to get her nails done and her hair styled. But for what? Pete was gone, and she was alone. Again. It was just her and her dreams, and the deadline for finding an internship was looming like a storm cloud.

Luckily, Joy had texted her with a message hoping she would see her there, and Garland actually responded. She had no date, she'd be hovering around her boss and her husband, and the only other people she'd know would be regulars from the coffee shop and maybe a few people from school. Seeing Joy would be nice—and a relief.

Snowflakes began to fall, fluttering down like winter moths and melting into the existing carpet of snow on the ground. Garland tiptoed through the drifts with her skirts in one hand and her high heels in the other, glad she'd worn her boots. Music billowed outside on the air every time someone opened one of the front doors.

She waited in line, greeted everyone with a smile, and when it was her turn at the coat check, peeled off her wrap and exchanged her boots for the dressy shoes. A few people around her gasped with delight, and she blushed. The blue dress looked stunning on her. It fit perfectly and the full tulle skirt glistened in the light.

She felt ridiculous like she was dressed up for prom, but the old high school flashbacks faded when she walked into the community center's recreational room. The Thorpes Chamber of Commerce had done an amazing job. The room was polka-dotted with decorated Christmas trees. They lined the walls and were surrounded with big puffy mounds of snow-like cotton drifts that glistened with delicate white lights. Sparkling white and blue bulbs crisscrossed the ceiling, creating a canopy of dreamy starlight. White tablecloths and chairs with lanterns and candles added more ambiance, and a refreshment table swathed in scarlet drapes and bows featured an ice sculpture and trickling chocolate fountain.

Garland gazed around the room with pleasure. Her mother had been on the ball's committee once upon a time. She would have loved it.

"You. Look. Amazing."

Garland turned with a grin. Mariah looked like a queen. "I look pathetic standing next to you. You look amazing in white." Garland stepped back to examine her friend's long, fitted gown. Her black hair was braided and coiled on her head like a Greek goddess. Beside her, Darren tugged at the neck of his green dress shirt.

"Looking pretty hot there, Darren," Garland teased. His belly strained at a black cummerbund.

"I feel stupid," groaned Darren. "We only do this once a year for you ladies, you know," he grumbled.

Mariah elbowed him. "This is the price you pay for spending New Year's on the couch watching football."

Garland snickered. She joined them on the edge of the room and turned to watch dancing couples move like tops across the floor. Glasses clinked and hushed conversations accentuated murmurs and the laughter of neighborly conversation.

Her heart swelled. This was Christmas. Friends and... A familiar figure caught her eye across the room. Tall and slender, her sister, Joy, waved from the dance floor. Garland's breath caught in her throat. She hadn't seen Joy since last summer when she dropped by for five minutes at the family Fourth of July picnic.

She smiled and waved back. Coming alone didn't look like it would be so bad after all. People were happy to see her, even if she felt lost inside. Someone touched her on the elbow, and she glanced back. Her almost-at-peace heart seized in her chest. It wasn't Darren on the other side of her arm. She almost coughed in surprise.

Pete Darling held out a hand. "May I have this dance?"

The room seemed to pause, and it felt like everyone was watching. The music had stopped. Speechless, Garland swallowed. He looked as handsome as ever. How could that be? She examined his trim, wide-shouldered form in the full black tuxedo, silk bow tie, and his coiffed, thick hair.

Pete's inviting hand waited, and she reached out to him just as the first strings of a slow waltz began to play. He pulled her onto the floor, and her dress swished around her. She felt beautiful. He was beautiful. For a brief moment, she wondered if Mariah was watching, and Joy, or maybe even her father if he'd come. This was better than a school dance. It was Christmas. With Pete Darling.

He wrapped an arm around her and drew her against his chest, and she had to force herself to concentrate on her feet so she didn't trip. His hand felt tingling warm and his arm around her back made her shiver. He smelled amazing.

Taking a deep breath, she forced herself to speak. "What are you doing here?"

He smiled at her. "I came back."

She felt her smile widen and lift her cheeks. "Another job to do?"

Something shifted in his dark, colorful eyes. "No more jobs."

"You're retiring?"

"Something like that."

She liked the way he sounded mysterious. Did that mean he would stay a little longer in Thorpes? She couldn't bring herself to ask.

They moved like they'd been dancing together for a lifetime. Garland knew instinctively when to step back, aside, or forward. The slightest pressure on her hand made her lift her arm so Pete could twirl her in a circle. It was a dream. The room spun by as if she were on a sparkling carousel. Garland felt like she was dancing around a thousand Christmas trees—or maybe it was just Christmas, she was circling back to, home again and filled with peace and happiness.

Feeling warmth on her cheeks, she glanced up through her lashes, wanting to cry and laugh and kiss him at the same time. His gaze had never left her. He watched her with an intensity she treasured as they came closer together and the music began to wind down like a music box. A slight breeze of disappointment blew over her, and she sighed. It was a moment she could have lived in forever.

She didn't resist when both his arms went around her in an intimate embrace. She looked up into his eyes. "How long will you be staying this time?" A faint warning voice in the back of her mind chided her. Did it matter? What did it mean? She had to find an internship. Her own time in Thorpes was coming to a close—the moment she'd dreamed of for years—ever since high school. Or was it, she thought with a start, really ever since the funeral? Her mind spun.

Pete tore his steady turquoise gaze away, whether unable or not wanting to answer, she wasn't sure. She thought he looked stricken. A soft touch on her shoulder made her turn.

"Garland?"

"Joy." Without having to think about it, Garland reached out and took her sister in a tight embrace. "Merry Christmas, Joy," she murmured, her heart swelling with happiness. "I am so happy to see you."

Suddenly, none of it mattered anymore. The anger, the bitterness, and the frustrations melted away. Joy, her father, the entire family... They hadn't meant to hurt her—they'd let her down, but it was done and in the past.

"Merry Christmas," laughed Joy. She pressed her cheek up against Garland's, and Garland wondered that they looked so different, her older sister taller with lighter hair and their dad's dark eyes.

Garland reached for Joy's hands and squeezed them. "I have something for you," she said shyly, "for Christmas. It's in the car, but first, let me introduce you to—" She looked back at Pete. He had a strange, alarmed look on his face like he was frozen under the lights and didn't know what to do.

She felt her face crack into a wide, amused smile. "This is—"

"Pete Darling!" Joy's eyes widened with delight.

Garland's introduction froze on her tongue. She swung her gaze back to Pete. He stared breathlessly.

Joy pushed past her and slung her arms around Pete's neck. "How are you, cousin? I haven't seen you in so many years!"

Garland stared. They seemed friendly. Too friendly.

"I'm fine," muttered Pete in an awkward silence.

Joy hesitated. "Garland, I didn't know you knew Pete."

"I didn't know you knew him either," she replied. Her mind burned with questions. She turned an accusing eye on him and stepped back.

"I," said Pete, and he shifted his gaze from her to the floor, "I met Joy years ago."

"At Mom's funeral," Joy explained. She studied Garland like she wondered if she knew.

"Oh," said Garland, pretending like she understood. Her mind whirled. "I ran into him at Aunt Grace's," was all she could offer.

"Yes, well, he's always around when a Darling needs him." Joy gazed up at him, her smile faint. "Thank you for helping with Mom's funeral expenses." She raised a brow at him. "I know it was you. You said you were a distant cousin and all, but as soon as you showed up, everything was paid for and then you disappeared."

"Yes," said Pete, blinking and in sudden control of himself, "but how are you, Joy? Your family?"

She grinned, "Oh, I'm on toddler number two, and we just bought our first home outside of town."

"I'm so happy for you." He smiled, but it looked terse. His gaze crept back over to Garland.

"And you're here with Garland?" This seemed to please Joy, but it made Garland flush. "You told me not to mention you were here last time, but you're here now with my sister?" Her tone sounded like she was teasing.

Garland took a step back, wanting to scream for someone to explain what was going on. As if sensing her suspicion, Pete reached for her hand again, but she pulled away.

His eyes pleaded with her, even as Joy rattled on about their brother's good luck getting a new job just when it seemed all was lost, and how Grace's new year's fees at the care home had been paid in full last week, and that Garland would be leaving soon to get an internship in the city.

When Garland heard her name, she tore her gaze away from Pete's stare, her heart thumping with sickening thuds in her chest. She looked down at his tanned hand on hers and jumped back to separate the connection between them.

"Yes," she said, interrupting her sister's banter, "I have to go now." She didn't know where or why.

Joy looked at her in surprise, but Garland backpedaled anyway, nearly tripping over her skirt hem. She almost crashed into Mariah and Darren. Her boss grabbed her elbow.

"What's wrong? You looked amazing out there."

Garland wheeled around and allowed a quick embrace. Her eyes crashed into Mariah's with a dead gaze. Before she could ask, Garland pulled away and lifting her skirts, hurried from the room and dashed out the front door, tripping through the snowdrifts in her stupid pointy shoes.

CHAPTER EIGHT

When Joy finally realized something was wrong, Pete snatched the opportunity to say, "I've been in town on a job." He shook her hand and forced a smile then hurried out of the ballroom after the girl in the indigo dress. She'd looked like a vision in the night sky, a beautiful sparkling constellation with rosy cheeks and a swan-like neck revealed by the drape of the French curls on the back of her neck. If it was so, her heart was the North Star.

He hurried out, pushing through the crowd with apologies, keeping the top of her tresses in his sights. His breath crystallized in the air as soon as he screeched to a halt outside the community center.

"Garland! Wait!" If she heard him, she didn't respond. She plowed through the snow with her skirts in her hands, leaving a trail of prints in the snow that looked like a fleeing reindeer. He hurried after her, the icy stuff sinking into his shoes between his socks. Nearly tripping over the curb, he slid to his knees but jumped back up to catch her before she reached a car in the parking lock and shook the handle.

"Garland!" He wanted to tackle her, roll with her across the magical glittering pure snow, but he restrained himself and reached for her elbow. "Please," he gasped. He realized he sounded like a pathetic, lost boy. He'd never begged, he thought with a shock, not for anything. He'd always had all he'd ever wanted, but this had no price. This girl he'd found was priceless, and he wanted her for himself. Forget the money. Forget the ancestry. Forget the deal.

"Garland," he choked. She turned, eyes wide and wet with tears. It felt like a cannonball in his gut.

"Who are you?" She shook off his grip on her elbow. "You know my sister, too?" Even in the dim light of the moon, he could see her cheeks glowed with anger and distrust.

"It's not what you think."

Her arms dropped to her sides with shaking fists. He waited for a pop on the side of the head. Struggling for breath, he held up his hands and shook his head.

"What are you doing to my family?"

He froze. It would sound impossible. Would she think him mad? "It's the inheritance." It was all he could tell her right now.

She furrowed her brows in a straight, angry line over her blazing glare. "Money?"

"Yes," he nodded. Pete stopped and took a deep breath now that he had her attention. "It's the money, your money. Your great-great grandmother's money."

"Wendy Pruitt?" Garland's tone sounded low and confused.

Pete realized she wanted to understand, but he could only tell her a little at a time. Too much at once would sound like a children's storybook. He shut his eyes for a moment, then opened them and took a deep breath. "Yes. Wendy Darling Pruitt. You see, if I tell you, I lose everything, but I'm okay with that now."

She stared. In that moment, she was a glistening, glowing, siren in blue taffeta, with creamy skin and a demanding gaze.

"I..." Pete felt his heart deflate. "It was me. I'm the person." He shook his head, trying to be truthful but not say too much right away. "I'm the ancestor, the relative who inherited all of the Darling money. You see, Wendy did leave all of her money to an orphan. I've had more than I needed, and I made a promise to... well, the family executors, that I would always make sure the Darlings were taken care of. It's in the provisions.

She swayed, and he reached out and took her in a tight embrace, staring into her eyes which looked open and curious.

"I have no family like I told you. There's no one, and so I've kept tabs on the family lines, all these years—and your family here in Thorpes."

"You paid for my mother's funeral?"

He nodded.

"The hospital bills?"

He bit his lip and nodded again.

"The Darling money was passed down to you? You're the benefactor," she said in a sluggish voice.

"I am," he admitted, his voice cracking. Telling was in breach of contract, one written in the stars. He was just a man now, a mortal man with a heart that wanted more than attention and appreciation, he wanted to be loved. And besides, he hadn't told her everything. Not yet.

"And my scholarships?" She sounded tense, and he tightened his embrace so she didn't run away again. She shivered.

"No, you earned them. You've earned everything." He gave a small chuckle. "You're the only Darling who never needed my help. Your school, your job, your little apartment... They're all yours. You've done it all yourself." He hesitated. "But you don't need to. I came here to see if you were okay, to see if you needed help with your tuition or future."

Garland pulled back with a jerk. "I don't need your help." Her eyes brimmed over with tears. "How could you... do such things without telling me?" She shook her head in distress.

"It's not like that. Your father doesn't know. Grace or anybody. Well, maybe Grace," he

admitted.

"She's not even here anymore."

"She remembers me," said Pete in a whisper. He couldn't even begin to explain. "But Joy, your sister," he hurried on, "she walked into the office at the funeral home and caught me there when your mother passed. I was supposed to be anonymous, but she got my name from the funeral director before I could leave, and a few years ago when I came to see Grace she saw me in the parking lot outside."

"So, Joy knows you."

"Not really. She knows I donated anonymously and thinks I'm a distant relative. We're acquainted, but only a little."

Garland seemed to be soaking it all in. "Then why did you come to the coffee shop? Were you spying on me?"

He gave her a faint smile and wished she could see the gut-wrenching love blossoming in his heart for her. "I wanted to check on the last Darling—the one who didn't need me—before I moved on."

"To where?" she said in a trembling whisper.

He shrugged. "I didn't know. My work in Miami is finished. I was watching over someone there, and your brothers and sisters are well. So maybe London or Colorado." He gave a pained, dry chuckle. "Garland, I don't know where I belong, but I want..." Before he could make himself say the words and tell her, she pushed him away.

"You're adopted. You're not even a Darling." A tear crested over her eye and streamed down her lovely cheek. "You're not one of us." She swallowed. "I don't know who you are, and I don't understand why you're really here, but we don't need or want your pity money."

It was like slapping him in the face. Pete stared, his throat in knots and his heart splitting into fissures and pieces. "I never saw it like that."

Garland tripped back and caught herself on the car. She jerked on the handle and scrambled inside before he could stop her, but he didn't intend to. She was right. He didn't belong in Thorpes. And he didn't belong to her either.

CHAPTER NINE

When Garland walked into the chilly apartment, she realized how small it looked now that it was empty. She set her gift bags on the small dinette table. Dad had given her a book on starting a small business, and Joy had brought a tin of homemade cookies. Her brothers had given her gift cards and wished her luck. It'd been a nice Christmas. Bittersweet.

Her throat tightened as her eyes watered. In fact, it was almost like old times with everyone there and the laughing, music, snacks, and goodies, except their mother wasn't there. Joy had set a framed picture of her on the table beside the nativity.

Garland sank down into the chair and rubbed her forehead. The apartment was packed except for a sleeping bag and her toiletries in the bathroom. Tomorrow would be a new day, an adventure, and a new life. She'd sent a deposit to a weekly live-in motel in Lawrenceburg until she could find a new apartment and a roommate. She would live a modest city life for now, until one of the bigger cities called.

She'd been waiting all her life. The tender sweet Christmas she'd shared with her family had healed old wounds. They'd welcomed her back with hugs, and things were looking up. She would be back for Easter, she promised, but even then her father had looked grieved. He'd sat beside her and patted her shoulder the entire time. They'd talked for hours. She made herself mention how much the sacrifice of being a caregiver for so long had really cost her, and he teared up and apologized. It was enough.

A movement near the front window snatched Garland out of her reflections, and she nearly screamed. Someone was in the apartment. She put a hand to her chest and gasped for air.

Bella Barrie, the giant pixie-looking woman, sat on the apartment's faded paisley couch filing a fingernail. She glanced over at Garland then went back to her work.

"Don't you knock?" It was all Garland could do not to shout. Bella didn't bother getting up. "How did you get in here?"

After a long, stewing pause, Bella lifted a dainty shoulder. "I have my ways." She raised the sharp metal fingernail file and waved it in the air.

"For heaven's sake!" Garland jumped to her feet wanting to look preoccupied. "Well, I'm busy in case you haven't noticed. I have to be out by tomorrow."

"Yes," mused the woman across the room, "your car looks like a clown car outside. Why don't you just hire a moving company?"

Garland grit her teeth. "Because," she said a loud voice, "I don't have that kind of money."

Bella shrugged again. "You could have," she whispered.

"What are you really doing here?" Garland pierced her with a gaze. She didn't want any reminders of Pete Darling. She'd run through so many labels for the man: con man, drifter, stalker, or player... but the truth of the matter was, she'd come to understand he was just a wealthy, generous, loyal, and lonely sincere man. His mouthwatering handsome grin and boyish playfulness were just perks... for somebody. But not her. She'd just been a job, an obligation, someone he was watching out for. Like she had her mother. It hurt he hadn't told her the truth.

"I had unfinished business up north," said Bella. She held her fingers out in front of her and examined them. "For some ridiculous reason, I started craving an iced and sugar-free vanilla latte with soy milk and a shot of salted caramel."

The sickening weight between her heart and stomach reasserted itself. Garland had pushed away the hopes she'd had for Pete, whatever they had been, as far away as she could while she'd packed up her apartment. She had deadlines to meet and goals to beat. All she needed was for this sulky secretary to go away.

"You won," she said in a sour voice. "Whatever it is you wanted, he left, and I'm going the other way. There's no reason for you to hang around and stand guard in Thorpes. No one's coming after your man."

Bella looked up in surprise. Her pale eyes widened, and she broke into sharp titters. Amused, she went back to filing the nails on her other hand. "He's not my man," she said in a choked voice of amusement. "He's just a boy really. A stupid boy that decided to grow up. Let's just say he's my boss—and my charge. I look after him."

"For who? The estate?"

"Something like that." She looked over with a pointed look. "He shouldn't have told you."

The gloomy light from outside must have lightened some, Garland thought, because even with the lamp off Bella seemed to glimmer and shine. She must have really been in love with Pete Darling no matter what she said.

"I asked him to accompany me," she continued in the cold silence. She glanced through the curtain sheers, "up north." She shivered. "It's cold here, and the people are... thick and loud." She made a noise of distaste.

Offended for herself and fellow New Englanders, Garland scowled. "So? What do you want from me?"

Bella put down the fingernail file. "Nothing," she said coolly. "In fact, he's miserable company. I've always been able to pull him away from people and things that weren't good for him, except for you stubborn Darlings, but he's a grown man now. And completely unhappy. Which makes me unhappy."

"I'll say so." Garland couldn't help the sarcasm. She stared, hoping for more.

"He's always been infatuated with the idea of a family," explained Bella. "First on his terms, but over time it became more... ordinary." She threw an accusatory glare at Garland. "Grace and your family have always been a distraction."

Garland couldn't help but admire Bella's beauty, even as she frowned.

"I should have never let him come to Thorpes again," Bella complained in a bitter tone. She pressed her bright red lips together to moisten them then tilted her head. "Like I said, he's just a boy to me, Garland. Once upon a time, I thought he always would be, but he chose to return here, I mean," she corrected herself, "to come to this country, and now there's nothing I can do to keep him from growing up—or believing in love. He's fallen head over heels for good this time, and I can't heal his little broken heart. No toys, no fun, no money."

Garland made a sarcastic noise. "His heart's broken? Why, because he can't secretly throw his money around anymore?"

"Oh, no," said Bella. "He's devastated. In the worst way."

Garland couldn't believe it. The very idea made her feel electric.

"The inheritance is gone. He's lost that." Bella grimaced. "He said too much. Broke the contract."

"He couldn't tell me?" Garland frowned in puzzlement.

Bella picked up the file and flicked it over a nail again. "There was a contract. One you couldn't begin to understand. He had access to the Darling money as long as he kept how and why he acquired it secret. He makes plenty enough of his own fixing those archaic flying machines, so he won't go hungry. Just, no more... Darlings." She stopped, and Garland thought she looked sad.

After a pause in which Garland was sure the woman knew her palms were sweating and trembling, Bella lifted a brow. "He'll never be happy again, not without you." She looked around the bare room with distaste. "Or this place."

"It reminds him of home," said Garland defiantly. "Thorpes reminds him of his past, whatever mysterious story that happens to be." Could it be true that Pete had honest feelings for her? More than for some charity case or out of compassion?

"Yes," said Bella with a hint of bitterness in her voice, "and you remind him of his future."

Garland's heart did a somersault at Bella's words. Was it true? Did he mean all of the attention he'd given her? The talks, the long looks, the soft touches, the kiss... Had it all been for real, because... She shook her head and her eyes brimmed over.

"You silly girl," said Bella, rising to her feet. "You've spent your entire life running around patching people up and making their lives better and loving every minute of it. You're just like him."

She picked up an expensive-looking handbag and dropped the file into it. "If you really think you'll find your happily-ever-after in some big city selling whatever you think is the next big thing, you do that, but I promise you," Bella gave her a firm stare, "you'll never find joy in an imaginary dream you made up to get away from your family or your mother's death. You might as well fly to another world. Besides," she gave another sharp shrug, "that coffee shop will go completely downhill after you leave."

Garland stared. She didn't want to leave, she never had, but she'd loved the idea of escaping from her pain, memories, the family, Christmas, and all of the happiness around her that she couldn't feel she could connect to anymore.

As if reading her thoughts, Bella nodded. "I asked Pete to pick up my drink. Of course, I had to convince him you wouldn't be there." She sighed. "If you don't mind, be a dear and run over to the Lava Java. He'll let it get cold."

Garland's heart felt like it was on fire, and she looked away so Bella couldn't see the emotions pouring out of her body and smeared all over her face. She realized it was hope, a burning desire, that Pete was in town, and she would see him again. She didn't know what to do about finding an internship, about the packed apartment, and whether she should go or stay. But the one thing she was sure of was that she wasn't Bella's servant. She looked up to give her a determined glare and refuse, but to her surprise, the woman had disappeared without a sound.

PETE STOOD AT THE END of the counter ignoring Mariah's stares. The café owner had nearly fainted when he'd walked in and quickly told him that Garland had already turned in her resignation. He'd nodded like he already knew, secretly relieved, because the pain would be too much to bear.

The holiday lights and evergreen boughs still draped around the café. Outside, the streets were frosted with thick blankets of knee-deep snow. Christmas music had been replaced, by soft, soothing jazz, but a holiday spirit still lingered. He sighed, leaned back against the counter with folded arms, and stared at his favorite table in the front corner.

Mariah came bustling out from the back and snuck a peek again. After handing a paper cup with a lid to Monty, she marched straight for Pete like a woman on a mission. His heart sank, and he stiffened.

She stopped in front of him and stared, her brown eyes drilling into his soul. "I'm pregnant," she announced.

Pete felt his eyes widen and forced down a laugh. "Congratulations?" Her accusatory tone confused him.

She looked around the café. "I can't run this place on my own anymore. We're three months behind, and I'm in debt up to my eyeballs."

His heart went out to her. Had Garland told her about the money? Was she asking for a bailout? "I'm sorry," he answered. She studied him, and he cleared his throat. "Is my hot chocolate ready yet?"

Mariah rolled her eyes. "You mean your New Year's supreme dark chocolate mint with cupcake crumbles? Do you know how long that takes to make?"

He raised a brow. "It's on the menu."

Mariah huffed. "That doesn't mean you have to order it."

"I'm sorry."

"You should be."

She gave him a funny glare, and he realized it was not the order she wanted him to be sorry about. How could he explain that his hands had been tied? His generous donations were to be done anonymously. Telling anyone the truth about the Darling inheritance and how he came into it would remove him as one of the executors. And it did. The London lawyers would take over now. He'd lost his cut, and the rest of the money would be doled out equally to everyone left.

This was it. The end of a fairytale even though he'd left out the details.

He grimaced and stared back out the window at the late afternoon sunshine reflecting off the snowdrifts. Garland would have left the café whether or not he'd come into her life anyway. It wasn't his fault. He hated the idea of the place shutting down though. Maybe he could help them out with some of his personal savings before he headed back to Florida to pack his things.

"Your cocoa," said Mariah from behind him. Pete turned about as she set it on the counter. Her voice sounded more patient now, forgiving. He glanced up to thank her, but instead of Mariah, he saw Garland standing behind her boss. His hand faltered on the counter, and he left it there, limp and stupid.

Mariah gave him a meaningful stare, hugged Garland, and then marched back to the kitchen. A saxophone crooned overhead. Only a few patrons read or sipped their drinks around the room.

Pete bit his lip. Garland's hair was up in its ponytail. Small, topaz earrings glittered from her earlobes. Her cheeks looked flushed, but he didn't know if it was because she'd just come in from the cold or because of him.

"Hi," he managed to say. He realized from her bright, round eyes she was nervous or afraid.

"I was just..." He struggled for an excuse. "Bella asked me to pick up her drink, and I..." He glanced up at the menu.

"You saw the January special and had to try it?"

Pete nodded sheepishly. A faint smile lifted the corners of Garland's mouth, and he hoped she didn't mind.

"You really should consider a sugar substitute," she said in a soft, teasing tone.

Pete balled his hand into a fist. The cocoa steamed between them.

"So, are you just passing through on a "job"?"

He looked up to see if she was being sarcastic, but she was watching him—almost breathlessly.

He gave a sharp shake of his head. "No," he whispered.

"Good." Her words pained him, and he looked away. "Actually," she continued, "when I heard you were around I wondered if you were the new tenant of my apartment."

He looked back in confusion. "No, I'd love to, but..." He studied her eyes. Did she really think he would try to move into her place when she moved out? That he was that creepy?

"Why not?" she asked.

He jerked in surprise.

Garland clenched her jaw as if she was scared of her question—or his reply. She cleared her throat. "I thought for a moment that you were coming here to live."

He stared. "Would that bother you?"

She looked back silently, her pulse throbbing in her neck. "No," she admitted in a whisper.

They stared at one another in silence. Pete wanted to jump over the counter, take her in his arms, beg her forgiveness, pour out his heart and all of the truths he'd had to keep secret... and kiss her.

"In fact," she said in a quiet voice, "I'm rethinking my brilliant move to Lawrenceburg with no job, no housing, no friends, and no family."

He swallowed. "You could do it," he said, unable to resist encouraging her. "You will be a success at whatever you choose to do in life, Garland. I know it."

"I believe I could and suddenly that's enough." She took a deep breath. "So, Mariah just told me there's an internship available this year for the Lava Java. A store manager—I'd report to the owner."

"To her?"

"Yes."

"She's having a baby," he said lamely.

Garland smiled. "I know, and I'm vain enough to think that this place won't make it without me."

He nodded. "They need you here."

She watched him then said in a whisper, "Do you think you'd be around?"

Pete's heart leapt up this throat, and he nearly called out, "I could be." Instead, he lowered his voice feeling shy and silly. "I want to be. Aunt Grace has offered me her home."

Garland nibbled her lip and watched him through lowered lashes.

"I'll stay," he promised.

Her eyes lit up, and Pete knew he had a chance. Not believed. Knew. He glanced down at the cocoa. He wasn't thirsty anymore. The sugar craving was gone. With a wave of hope, he moved the cup aside and jumped over the counter.

Garland burst out into nervous laughter. "What are you doing, Pete, you're going to spill that every—"

He muffled her outburst with his lips over hers, and she caught him up in a kiss, her arms circling around his neck and pulling him closer. For a moment, Pete thought he could fly.

ROUNDS OF CLAPPING echoed in the kitchen as Garland led Pete through the back. "Are you taking the internship?" Mariah demanded.

Garland stopped, her heart pounding in her ears, her body trembling, and with tears in the back of her throat. Pete kept his arm right around her, and she gave him a squeeze just to let him know she relished his warmth and closeness. "I'm taking the internship," Garland announced.

Doug and the rest of the small staff cheered. Mariah beamed. "I knew I could count on you."

"Thank you, and I'm glad," Garland giggled, "because I hope I can count on you since I need a place to live for a few weeks."

"No problem." Her boss grinned at her. "Are you going to get your old place back?"

Garland looked over at Pete and grinned when he met her eyes. "No, it already has an interested tenant. I thought I'd take your spare room while I look for a place close to my dad's house."

Mariah beamed. "That's awesome. I knew it would all work out."

"Did you?" teased Pete. He tweaked Garland's waist, and she couldn't keep the happiness off of her face.

Mariah shrugged. "She likes making sweets. You like drinking them."

Pete laughed. "You have me there. It's true, especially during the holidays. Oh, and by the way, I'd wish you all a Merry Christmas, but I'm too late."

"You're never too late," chided Garland. She took him by the hand and led him out into the snow-covered street. Festive lights gleamed overhead, lighting the night with the promise of a new year and a new life. They stopped under a sagging bough filled with ribbon and mistletoe.

"My first real Christmas," mused Pete, "in a long time."

She grinned at him. "It's my new favorite holiday," she said then ducked her head shyly.

Pete lifted her chin with his finger just as another curtain of snowflakes began to fall from the sky. "Merry Christmas, Garland Tate. I have so many things to tell you."

Heart dancing to a happy tune, Garland looked up into his faraway turquoise eyes. "Merry Christmas, Pete, darling."

EPILOGUE

The quaint yellow home on Tiger Lily Drive was the perfect home for Thorpes' newest airport mechanic and the Lava Java's manager. Pete and Garland Darling moved into their great aunt's home the summer after she passed away, although the residents at the Pine Grove retirement home claimed Grace Darling Hale never died at all, but flew away into the night in her pajamas, singing and laughing as she glided right toward a morning star.

The neighbors soon decided that Mr. Darling had a penchant for proper English gardening, and his wife decorated the yard with garden gnomes that many saw wink along with the fireflies on late summer evenings.

Privy to one another's secrets, and totally and happily in love, Garland Darling chose to celebrate their second Christmas together with a simple fir tree decorated with fairies, mermaids, and forest animals. Pete chose white twinkling starry lights and insisted on strings of candy as garland to wrap around the branches.

"What's this?" he asked, as he stepped behind the tree to wrap around his sweet trimmings. He leaned down and examined a bright red and gold box tucked under the tree branches.

Garland stepped out of the kitchen. An apron fit snugly over her small baby bump, and her cheek was dusted with flour. "Oh," she said with a sheepish grin. "That's your Christmas present, but you just might want to wait."

His bright eyes lit up like a little child's. "I can't wait. It's my first real Christmas and that makes this my first real present."

Garland laughed. "If you open it now, the surprise will be ruined."

"I love surprises," Pete admitted, but he dropped down to his knees and picked up the perfectly square box anyway. "I hate to wait though. You never know what tomorrow will bring."

"Yes," teased his wife, "you could be kidnapped by pirates or Bella could show up at our door."

He raised his chin. "Never underestimate the element of surprise when it comes to fairies." He picked up the box and shook it, and Garland crossed the room. She collapsed onto the small sofa with a smile. "If you can't wait, open it then. You have me all excited now." She grinned and bit her lip, and he tore his gaze from hers and looked down.

"If you say so," he said, and Garland laughed.

Pete picked up the gift and eased around the tree to slip down onto the couch beside her.

"What do you think it is?"

"A cocoa mug? A key to the café?"

"No, but nice guesses." Garland smiled even wider.

Pete turned it over in his hand then in a burst of excitement, pulled the red ribbon off and pulled open the box. Garland watched as he dug around in tissue and then pulled out a glittery pink airplane.

His brows wrinkled. "What's this?"

Garland grinned. "It's a Christmas ornament. I thought you'd like to open your daughter's first one."

His mouth dropped open, and his eyes teared up. "My daughter? It's a girl?"

"Yes. I thought this would be a suitable ornament for a girl whose daddy can teach her how to fly."

Pete's eyes teared up, and he leaned over and gave Garland a long embrace. With his chin on her shoulder, he gazed into the twinkling tree, a thousand memories passing through his mind. "All you need is faith and trust," he whispered.

His wife finished the story for him. "And a little bit of pixie dust."

THE END

MORE BOOKS BY DANIELLE THORNE

<u>Contemporary Romance</u>[1]
<u>The Doctor's Christmas Dilemma</u>[2]
<u>A Home For The Twins</u>[3]
<u>A Promise For His Daughter</u>[4]
<u>His Daughter's Prayer</u>[5]
<u>Falling For The Coach</u>[6]
<u>The Cottage Swap</u>[7]
<u>Holiday Romance</u>[8]
<u>Brushstrokes and Blessings</u>[9]
<u>Henry's Holiday Charade</u>[10]
<u>Valentine Gold</u>[11]

---

1. http://www.daniellethorne.com

2. http://www.daniellethorne.com

3. http://www.daniellethorne.com

4. http://www.daniellethorne.com

5. http://www.daniellethorne.com

6. http://www.daniellethorne.com

7. http://www.daniellethorne.com

8. http://www.daniellethorne.com

9. http://www.daniellethorne.com

10. http://www.daniellethorne.com

11. http://www.daniellethorne.com

<u>Historical Romance</u>[12]
<u>The Gentlemen of the Coast Series</u>[13]
<u>A Most Improper Introduction</u>[14]
<u>The Privateer of San Madrid</u>[15]
<u>A Pirate at Pembroke</u>[16]
<u>Proper Attire</u>[17]
<u>Georgia Bride</u>[18]

---

12. http://www.daniellethorne.com

13. *http://www.daniellethorne.com*

14. *http://www.daniellethorne.com*

15. *http://www.daniellethorne.com*

16. *http://www.daniellethorne.com*

17. *http://www.daniellethorne.com*

18. *http://www.daniellethorne.com*

ABOUT THE AUTHOR

Danielle Thorne writes happily-ever-afters set in the South for Harlequin Love Inspired. A graduate of BYU-Idaho, she also writes stories about Regency ladies, pirates, and not-so-distressed damsels from her home south of Atlanta. Free time is filled with documentaries, too much yard work, and not enough travel. When not writing wholesome romances, Danielle hangs out with friends or chases cats. She enjoys the outdoors and serving in her church and community. Danielle's been married to the same fellow for thirty years, has four sons, four daughters-in-law, and grandbabies. She loves them more than life.

Visit the author at http://www.daniellethorne.com.

Don't miss out!

Visit the website below and you can sign up to receive emails whenever Danielle Thorne publishes a new book. There's no charge and no obligation.

https://books2read.com/r/B-A-RXHB-PLSCB

Connecting independent readers to independent writers.

www.ingramcontent.com/pod-product-compliance
Lightning Source LLC
Chambersburg PA
CBHW031433150726
47989CB00002B/927